My Father's Son

Ryan S. Pack

This book is dedicated to everyone
that can look at the stars and still see
the magic, not just the science. Just
because you can't see it doesn't mean
 it isn't there.

"Cattle die, kinsmen die; the self must also die. I know one thing which never dies: the reputation of each dead man." — Hávamál, Stanza 77

Chapter One

It was cold standing in the grove of trees, and my pants were wet from mid-thigh down.

Also, I was getting pretty pissed off.

I was hunkered down behind the trunk of an old oak, straining to see through the foggy half-light thrown by the single bulb of the entrance light of my dorm about fifty yards away. The man was still standing there, leaning against the wall as if he had all the time in the world. He looked like the kind of man that would have no compunction whatsoever about standing there until Judgment Trump, if that were needed. I was cold, wet, hungry, and like I said, getting pissed.

I'm not used to hiding in the tree line to escape the notice of strangers standing in my dorm's entrance. I'm not used to hiding from anyone at all. At six foot, seven inches and two hundred and sixty-five pounds of muscle, I've never felt the need to hide from anyone. If anything, I've had a few people hiding from *me* at time or two. So, this new development was disconcerting, to say the least.

The man standing in the entrance made me look like an underfed Third World orphan. He was easily seven feet tall and so wide across the shoulders that he would have had to turn sideways to walk through the door he was guarding. He had honey-blonde hair that was pulled back into a braid that fell the length of his massive back. He was wearing faded Levis and a Navy pea coat over a t-shirt that proclaimed "Death before Dishonor" emblazoned in scrollwork over a screaming eagle. He had on a pair of scuffed combat boots that looked like they had seen plenty of action. He had a beard, neatly trimmed and about a shade or two darker than his hair. Although appearing relaxed, he gave off a sense of watchfulness and tension; as if he was ready to uncoil and strike with deadly effect. He looked, in a word, like a badass.

I had first noticed him earlier in the day, when I was heading from my World Civilizations class to Public Speaking II, a class I despised. Even from across the campus, he was a sight. He looked as out of place as an evergreen in the desert, and the flow of humanity that was passing across the quad should have been doing double-takes by the hundreds, but no one even glanced at him. Whenever someone got close enough to him, they would simply detour around him, never looking his direction. At times, people would jostle each other in their haste to go around him. I could understand the feeling of not wanting this man angry at you for bumping into him, but the fact that no one so much as glanced at him confused me. My confusion turned to a jolt of fear when I realized that he was staring straight at me.

Fear is not something that I am accustomed to. My size and general disposition preclude it as an emotion that is high on my daily activities roster. Most people I've met tend to feel the same way about me that I was feeling about this hulking giant across the quad. That arrow of fear shot through me, leaving me angry and confused. I squared my shoulders and began to walk towards the man, intent on asking just what in the hell he was looking at. It was right about then I noticed that he was angling straight for me, as well.

I did an about-face and practically fled to my class.

I sat in class for an hour, fuming about the sudden loss of courage I had exhibited on the quad. I seethed. It felt like electricity was snapping off of me in little jolts. My classmates must have felt it, because they all scooted just as far away from me as they could, given the fact we were packed into the auditorium-sized room. I ground my teeth and exhaled through my nose like an angry bull. Finally, halfway through the lecture, my professor had stopped and asked me if I was all right. Feeling embarrassed, I told him yes, I was fine. I just had a headache. I slumped in my desk to make myself smaller in the hope I would attract less attention and made a mental effort calm myself down.

It was less than a stellar success.

When class ended, I stalked out of the room, no less angry than when I had entered it. I turned towards the stairway on the right, which would bring me out closest to my dorm and there he was. He was just standing at the foot of the stairs looking up at me. Again, I turned and headed in the opposite direction without even thinking. I was down the hallway and halfway down the opposite staircase before I had even registered what I was doing. That made me even angrier.

Instead of going to my dorm to study, I headed to my favorite bar. I spent the next four hours drinking pitcher after pitcher of beer, morosely wishing I could get drunk. I can never seem to get there, no matter how much I drink. I've always attributed it to my size. I just can't seem to get a sufficient amount of booze into my system quickly enough to do anything more than catch a slight buzz. This talent was marveled at by my friends, who would take bets from suckers that I could out-drink any three of them. Wonderful talent, believe me. All I'm able to do is spend far more money than anyone else on booze, and never get the same enjoyment from it.

I suppose I should take a moment and say a bit more about myself than the fact that I'm an incredibly talented drinker. My name is Alexei Addison. Everyone just calls me Alex. I'm twenty-three years old, and a second-year college student at the University of Kentucky. I plan on becoming a lawyer, if my grades and my finances hold out. My parents aren't exceptionally wealthy, just a couple of blue-collar Americans hacking out their piece of the American Dream. My maternal grandparents emigrated here from Russia in 1949, after World War Two. My paternal grandparents were both killed during the siege of Stalingrad. My grandparents would often tell me about how they had managed to cross the border into West Berlin before the Iron Curtain slammed down across the continent. They were some of the lucky few that made it out before the U.S.S.R effectively closed the door shut to the West.

My parents had me late in life. I was a bit of a surprise to them, I think. Not that they don't love me, because they do. It's just that after being married for twenty-four years, you don't really expect a kid to pop in on you. They're in their mid-60's now, almost ready to retire. I love them dearly, but I think that they breathed a sigh of relief when I graduated high school and headed off to college. I just don't think they knew exactly what to make of this giant that their loins had produced.

My mom said I got my size from her side of the family, that some of her uncles had been huge. You'd never know it to look at her though. She's a tiny little thing, always flitting around the house like a hummingbird. My dad isn't much bigger. I was a full foot taller than him when I was eleven. Our small house in Columbia, Kentucky just didn't seem to be able to contain me. I was always smashing into things. Columbia is a tiny town. Its only real claim to fame is that Jesse James robbed the bank there on April 29, 1872 and killed the cashier.

I played football for Adair County High School so I could get a college scholarship. I got the scholarship, but it didn't quite work out for me at the University of Kentucky. I was kicked off the team after my second game when I broke an opposing lineman's jaw. That in and of itself isn't enough to get you kicked off the team, but I broke the lineman's jaw after the play. I ripped his helmet off and cold-cocked him on the line of scrimmage. I couldn't help myself. The guy pissed me off, so bang goes the scholarship. I've been getting by on financial aid packages and student loans, and I work part-time on the tobacco farms outside of town. It's tight, and I live on a lot of Ramen noodles and peanut butter. All told, I'm pretty content here at U.K., and I figure that I'll get my law degree, if only so I can pay back all the damn student loans.

"Content" did not describe my current condition, however. Standing in the cold with wet legs (I had stepped into what I thought was a small puddle of water, only to find it was a pothole about a foot deep) behind an oak tree at ten o'clock at night isn't my idea of contentment. I hadn't pissed before leaving the bar, either, and I had what felt like two gallons of beer settling in my bladder like a lead weight.

I was mustering up my courage to walk out and confront the giant in my doorway when he stopped me dead by turning in my direction and saying, "Alexei, are you going come out sometime tonight, or are you just going stand there until you piss yourself?"

Okay, everybody out of the pool.

My surprise and anger finally turned out to be stronger than my inherent and altogether unnatural fear of this man, and I tore out of the tree line and stomped towards him. *Hell with it*, I thought, *If he rips my head off, at least I won't have to piss so badly.*

He didn't move, but stood there quietly as I marched towards him. When I had made into the pool of dim light thrown off by the entrance bulb, he slowly straightened from his leaning pose. My anger took a momentary leave of absence, but fear was right there to step into the gap. This guy was huge. I wasn't accustomed to looking up at anything but the sky, but I had to crane my neck to look him in the face. I swallowed hard and pressed on. I just didn't see anything else to do. If this guy wanted me, so be it, here I was. I stepped to within arm's reach of him and stood with my hands on my hips. Looking him in the eye was one of the most difficult things I've ever had to do. Every fiber of my being was screaming like a mad bastard for me to get the hell away from this guy, and to do it yesterday.

I stood my ground, though, and in my toughest voice I said, "All right. Here I am. You know my name, but I don't have the first clue who the hell you are. So, what's your problem? You've been stalking me all day. What do you want, a kiss or something? I don't swing that way, sweetheart."

I was proud of myself for getting my little speech out without any noticeable waver in my voice. At least I *was,* until I watched the man's eyes change.

They were brilliant blue, the color of the sky near sunset. When I made my smart-ass comment, they flattened and turned to glacial ice. His face was so grim that I could feel my insides weaken. *Way to go,* I thought, *you've just earned yourself about three months in the hospital, if you're lucky.* But then his face relaxed, and he threw back his head and laughed. His eyes went back to their normal shade of calm blue and he stuck out his hand.

"My name's Henry Dall, Alexei. Or should I call you Alex?"

I had been raised to believe that you shook the hand of the Devil if he offered it to you, out of simple good manners. However, I don't think that the Devil has hands that looked like the business end of a bear. Putting my own hand into his, I said, "I don't care if you call me Barbara, just as long as you don't crush my hand."

He laughed again and shook my hand. His grip wasn't just iron, it was steel. It felt like he could have bent Wolverine's claws into pretzels if he had taken the notion to. But he was gentle enough, and I received my hand back only slightly bruised and tingly. He flipped his head towards the entrance and said, "Let's go to your room. I've got some things we need to discuss."

"Not a chance", I said flatly. "I'm not about to invite you up to my room so you can murder me in front of my friends. Let's just kill me down here where it's nice and private, okay?"

He gave me that cold glance again. "If I wanted to kill you, you would be well and truly dead. Now, *ya opazdyvayu*. So, *da*, we're going up to your room. Got me?"

My mind kicked into overdrive. I wasn't fluent in Russian, but I had picked up a bit from my grandparents. Henry had just told me he was running late, and he had done so in a way that let me know that he was aware of not only my name, but that I came from a Russian family. Oh, and also, he seemed to know how badly I needed to piss. Still, all weirdness aside, there was just enough smart-ass left in me that I wasn't going to take orders from a Sasquatch in a pea coat. I slowly held up both hands and flipped him off. "Suck it, big boy. I'm not inviting you to my room. I will, however, invite you to go fuck yourself."

I was mentally prepared for the ass-beating I was about to receive, but not for what actually happened. Henry Dall seemed to swell in front of me. His seven feet turned into about nine, and his clothes seemed to shift somehow. His pea coat and jeans turned, just for a second, into something else, but I couldn't register what it was. When he spoke, his voice sounded like the boom of a cannon.

"Your room. Now. Don't push your luck, little brother."

I was past him and holding open the door so he could enter before I realized that I had moved. Turning sideways to accommodate his shoulders, he stalked past me and into the foyer. To my ultimate happiness, he was back to his normal size and attire. I said nothing else as we made our way up to my room, although I was mentally berating myself for acting like a coward in front of this guy. I was receiving a first-class lesson in humility, it appeared.

I had the room to myself, since my former roommate had flunked out during the last semester and no one had taken his place yet. This was for the best, since I would have had a hard time explaining Henry Dall to anyone had they been there. We walked in and he flopped down in my recliner. Looking perfectly at home, he asked if I had anything to drink. I went to the tiny refrigerator I kept in my room and pulled out two bottles of Guinness Extra Stout. I handed him one and was reaching for the bottle opener when he flipped the cap off with his thumb like a tiddly-wink. I shook my head and used the opener on my own bottle and sat down on the edge of my bed. We sat like that for a few minutes until the silence got to be oppressive.

"I thought you said you were running late for something. Here we are. So, talk. What do you want?"

Henry looked around the room. It was a mess, but housekeeping was never one of my strong suits. His glance fell on a poster on the wall. It was a mock motivational poster, like the ones you see in libraries. They usually had some breath-taking scenic view of mountains or oceans with phrases like "A journey of a thousand miles begins with a single step." Crap like that. Mine was of Thor holding a hammer over his shoulder. The caption underneath said "Your god was nailed to a cross. My god carries a hammer. Any questions?" Henry looked at it for a moment and then chuckled.

"What? You don't dig my décor?" I asked.

He shook his head. "My father would rip that thing off the wall, crumple it up, and make you eat it", he said.

"Your dad a Christian?"

"Something like that." He grinned. "Let's just say he doesn't approve of making light of religion. *Any* religion. He's a bit zealous about it, to tell the truth."

I shrugged. "Well, I guess it's a good thing he's not here to be offended then, isn't it?"

Henry gave me another long look. After several uncomfortable minutes, he sighed and said, "Well, you've got courage, I'll give you that. I figured you might not have enough. I thought maybe the blood was too thin."

I looked at him incredulously. "Do you mind telling me just what the fuck you are talking about? Because let me tell you something, big boy, I've had about all the bullshit I'm willing to put up with for one night. Now you can kick the hell out of me if you want to, or pull that jacked-up David Copperfield routine with your clothes again, but enough is most definitely enough."

To my relief, he didn't get angry, or swell up like Mr. Toad of Toad Hall. He just sat there a few minutes, stroking his beard. Finally, after what seemed like forever, he looked at me. When he spoke, his voice was soft, almost a whisper.

"Tell me what you know about your family."

Of all the things I had been expecting, this wasn't one of them. "My family", I stuttered, "What about my family?"

"What do you know about them? Where are they from, that sort of thing?"

I scratched my head and looked at the floor. This was going from weird right into frigging creepy. A giant in a pea coat stalks me across campus, turns into some sort of sidewalk magician, and then asks me about my family history. There's a limit to the amount of weirdness a person should have to deal with. I looked up at him and told him quietly, "I have no intention of talking to you about my family. They aren't any of your business. If you are threatening me in some way about my family, trust me when I say this: I will do my dead-level best to kill you right here, right now".

"I don't give a shit how big you are. You scare me, I admit that. I don't remember ever being scared of anyone before, but you scare the hell out of me. Regardless, if you try to fuck with my family, I *will* kill you. Believe that."

Again, he surprised me by not flying into a rage. Instead, he nodded; as if that was the answer he was looking for. He smiled at me, and for a moment I was disarmed by the pure friendliness of the gesture. I found myself smiling back a little. What the hell was going on?

"Listen", he said, "I have nothing against your family, and I'm not here to threaten them in any way. In fact, I am here for quite the opposite. If anyone tried to hurt your family, they would find themselves in a serious world of pain. You can rest assured that your family is safe. I wouldn't let anyone harm them. You have my oath upon that."

The odd formality of his words and the sincerity I saw in his eyes was enough to convince me that he was telling the truth. His use of the word "oath" was riveting. It wasn't a word he seemed like he would use lightly.

I found myself telling him what I knew about my family, which wasn't much. I finished up by telling him about my grandparents flight from East Berlin after the war ended, their emigration to the United States, and my parents' lives in Columbia. He sat quietly through all this, stroking his beard and listening. When I was finished, he stared off into space for a few moments, and then turned back to me.

"Okay, Alex. How are you with suspension of disbelief?"

I was flummoxed again. "*What?*"

He smiled. "Suspension of disbelief. The ability to consider things that normally you would find impossible to believe. I guess I'm asking if you're capable of believing in things that you cannot see. Taking things on faith." He gestured at my poster. "That pretty much tells me that you're not a Christian. Do you have any religious beliefs at all, or are you an atheist?"

Damn. First a family history lesson, and now a theological discussion? What next, a debate over abortion? I shook my head. "I don't know, Henry. To be perfectly honest, I don't really think about it. I suppose I'm an agnostic. I just don't know one way or the other. Some days it all seems like one big cosmic joke, and the some days I feel like there has to be something to it all, that it can't just be an accident. Why are you asking me all this for? Dude, no offense, but you are one seriously fucked-up individual."

He just nodded again, as if that was just what he expected me to say. "So, an agnostic, but with doubts about it. You're sitting on the fence pretty hard there, little brother."

"Why do you keep calling me that? You trying to tell me that my dad's been going around the country planting giants? 'Cause I don't buy it, buddy. My dad loves my mom. Besides, if you saw my dad, you'd know just how much crap that is. He's little, man. I mean, like, *tiny*."

Henry shook his head. "No, I'm sure your father loves your mother very much. Besides, this doesn't have anything to do with your father's side of the family anyway. It's your mother's side that I'm speaking of."

I tossed my hands up. "Oh, so you're my long-lost big brother that my mom had on the side but kept from my dad, right? Come on, Henry, this is bullshit."

He grinned again. "No, your mother has exactly one child, and that's you. I'm talking about her side of the *family*, not her in particular."

I gave up. "All right. That's it, everybody just take five and head for the showers. Either you start making some sense, or I'm going to have to ask you to leave, Henry. To quote Yoda: 'Up with this shit I will not put'."

Henry sat back into the recliner and looked at the ceiling for a few minutes. With a sigh, he said, "Okay. But there's a reason for my questions. And I really do need to know about your ability to accept things you can't explain. It's relevant, whether you realize it or not. Can you accept things that you can't logically explain?"

I thought for a moment. "Sure, I guess so. I mean, I've never seen a UFO or the Loch Ness Monster, but that doesn't mean they don't exist. They say there's another planet out past Pluto. I haven't seen *that*, but I don't just automatically deny its existence. But what the hell does any of this have to do with the price of beans in Paraguay?"

He leaned forward, the recliner's springs giving a tortured squeal. "It's important that you keep an open mind. What I'm about to tell you, and then show you, is going to be so far beyond your belief curve that you might become a bit unhinged by it, and I don't want that. Do you understand me?"

I was beginning to get nervous. What the hell was this guy's deal? "All right, an open mind, check. I've got it. I'm open to anything you throw at me, big guy. Bring it on."

He looked closely at me, his eyes boring into mine. It was disconcerting, but I managed to hold his gaze. "All right, Alex. What I'm about to tell you is going to tax your imagination a bit, and your first instinct will be to tell me to go 'fuck myself' again. However, hear me out completely. Everything I'm about to tell you is true, and I can and will prove it. But no interruptions until I've finished. Deal?"

I nodded. "Sure. You got a deal. I'm mute." I sat back on the bed, reclining on my elbows and looked at him. "The floor is all yours, Henry."

He stood up and I was again amazed at his size. His head nearly brushed the ceiling. *He must have a hell of a time with ceiling fans*, I thought. He began to pace back and forth in front of me, his hands clasped behind his back. His eyes had taken a far-off cast and when he spoke, it was almost as if he were talking to himself instead of me.

"First off, my name isn't really Henry Dall. That's just what I go by when I'm here." He saw my eyebrows rise in a question and held up one hand. "Not until I'm finished, remember?" I nodded for him to continue. "Do you know anything about the Norse civilization, beyond that poster or comic books?"

I shrugged. "Yeah, a little bit. I did a report on the Vikings back in high school. Got an 'A' on it, too."

He nodded. "Okay, then. So you know about the Norse gods, right? Can you name any of them?"

I thought for a minute, trying to remember that long-ago report. "Let's see… there's Odin, he's the main god. There's Thor, of course, everybody knows him. There's Loki…"

He cut me off with a brusque wave of his hand. "Loki is *not* one of the gods, Alex."

I shrugged again. "Sorry. Jeez, if I had known there was gonna be a quiz, I'd have studied. Uh, there's Freya, Friday is named after her… or is Friday named after Freyr? I can't remember, really. I know Thursday is named after Thor, and Tuesday is named after Tyr, and there was another day named after somebody…"

"You're thinking of Wednesday. It's named after Odin."

I stared at him. "That doesn't make any sense. It would be 'Odinsday', not 'Wednesday'."

"Odin is also known as 'Woden'. Does that make more sense?"

"Yeah, I can see that. Uh… look, it was a long time ago, and I can't really remember any more than that."

"Do you remember Bifrost?"

"Oh, yeah, sure. Bifrost was the Rainbow Bridge. It linked Asgard and uh…whatever they called earth. Something-gard."

"Midgard."

"Yeah, that was it. Midgard. And there was something about a tree with a funny name. Like I said, it was a long time ago. Why the hell are we talking about the Norse gods, anyway?"

Henry held up his hand again. "Not until I'm done, remember?"

I gestured for him to go on.

"All right. On Bifrost there is the hall of Heimdall, Himinbjorg, the Cliffs of Heaven. Heimdall is the watchman of the gods. It's his job to guard Bifrost and warn the Aesir of trouble or attack."

"Who are the Aesir?"

He gave me a disgusted look. "And you got an '*A*' on this paper of yours? The Aesir are the Norse gods. Anyway, Heimdall's other job is to blow his horn Gjall to warn of the coming of Ragnarok. Tell me you at least know what *that* is."

"Sure. The big be-all, end-all fight at the end of time. Kind of like Armageddon."

He snorted. "Yes, 'kind of like Armageddon'. The end of all that is, was, or will ever be. The Doom of the Gods." His eyes regained that far-off cast. "It will be horror unlike anything that has ever been seen before. All that is will fall into fire and ash. The earth will crumble, and the gods themselves will die."

"Sounds like a pretty picture. How, exactly, can a *god* die, anyway? Isn't that a contradiction of terms?"

He shook his head, as if to clear it. "There are ways. It doesn't matter. Not yet, anyway. I was telling you about Himinbjorg, the hall of Heimdall. He sees everything that moves on Midgard. He can hear the grass growing, the sound of a sheep's wool rubbing against its skin. He is the perfect watchman, because he never sleeps. Which is a royal pain in the ass, let me tell you."

I chuckled. "Yeah, I would imagine it would be. I feel for the poor guy. I mean, if he was real. Never being able to sleep? Man... that would bite the banana."

Henry stopped pacing and looked at me. His eyes still had a distant cast, and his voice was gentle when he spoke.

"It does bite the banana. Trust me. And thank you for your sympathy. I appreciate it."

I just stared at him with a confused look on my face. "What sympathy? What are you taking about?"

He smiled at me again. "Alex, my name isn't Henry. I am Heimdall, the Watchman of the Gods."

My voice failed me and I could only stare at him.

Chapter Two

"You're Heimdall? Like the *god* Heimdall? Live on a bridge that's a rainbow and keep a look-out for all the Norse gods? Sure, Henry, no problem. Oh, since we're sharing and all, *my* name is actually Zeus, and I'm bad for flinging lightening at folks when they piss me off."

He just stood there with his arms folded across his chest. "Where's that open mind you promised me?"

"Hold on a second, big guy. I'm all about an open mind, but I figured you were going to tell me something like we're related from good old Mother Russia, or I'm actually the only surviving member of the Romanov family or something like that. I can keep an open mind about that, but this… sorry, man, but this is just too much on the bullshit side to swallow."

"When we were downstairs and I told you that we were going to come up here, you opened that door in a hurry. Why did you do that? What was that David

Copperfield comment, hmmm? Why did you suddenly have a change of heart and invite me up here so quickly?"

I sat up in the bed, nervous again. "Look, Henry, I've had a lot of beer tonight. I mean a *lot*. Sure, I *thought* I saw something downstairs, but it was just my beer goggles, you know? Nothing more than that."

"You sound like Ebenezer Scrooge. 'There's more of gravy than of grave about you'. You remember how that wound up, don't you?"

I was getting more uncomfortable by the second. I was in a very small room with a very big man that was obviously in need of some serious counseling.

"Look, Henry…"

"My name is Heimdall." He said it quietly, but with great force.

"Okay, okay… *Heimdall*, then. Look, I don't mean to upset you, or anything. I don't make it a point of going out of my way to piss off people that look like they can pull my arm off like a Thanksgiving turkey drumstick, but what you're saying is just… well, it's just not possible, man. I mean, yeah, you look like the kind of guy I would want guarding my place while I was sleeping and all, but you're not a god, dude. You're bad-ass and you look mean as hell, but you ain't a god. I hate to pop your bubble, but that stuff doesn't actually hold water. There's no such thing as the Norse gods, especially Norse gods that go around quoting Dickens and seem to be invisible to anyone but me. There are no gods. They're just myths, you know?"

He smiled. "I happen to like Dickens, and I have plenty of time on my hands to read. Insofar as no one seems to be able to see me, they can, it's just that my… well, *otherness* makes it difficult for them to process me, so they sort of shut me out, mentally. And my companions will be very upset when I tell them that they aren't real."

"Ha, ha, very funny. Look… this has gone about as far as I'm willing to go with it, okay? You wanted to come up and talk, and we have. I listened to you, like I said I would. But that's it. It's late, and I'm tired. So if you don't mind, I'm gonna get some sleep. You want to talk some more, hey, we'll grab a beer tomorrow afternoon after my classes let out. How does that sound? I like you. I didn't think I would at first, but I kind of do now. You're funny, and I'll bet you're a complete riot when you get some booze in you. But no more tonight. I'm all done in. Okay?"

He shook his head. "All right. I didn't actually figure you would just believe me outright. I don't suppose anyone would. So, are you ready for the suspension of disbelief I talked about? This is going to be pretty unnerving, so try not to scream, okay? You'll frighten the other guys in the dorm, and there's no reason for that. If you feel like you've got to scream, do it into your pillow, all right?"

I was definitely getting freaked out now. To pacify him, I reached behind me and picked up my pillow. I held it up to him and said, "Okey-dokey. I'm ready to roll. Astound me."

He stood stock-still in the center of the room for a moment, his head lowered. He took a deep breath and looked down at me. As had happened downstairs, his whole body seemed to shiver for a second. It was like looking at someone through the flames of a fire, or a heat mirage floating up from a hot pavement road. He swelled and once again he stood at least nine feet tall. His head should have went right through the ceiling, but for some reason it didn't. His pea coat turned into a long leather tunic covered in chain mail, and he was wearing leather breeches. A helmet appeared on his head, and there was a huge sword suddenly strapped to his belt. His bare forearms were now covered in metal bracers with intricate knot work designs on them. His neatly clipped beard flowed out and fell halfway down his chest, and the braid that had been holding his hair snapped, sending his long hair flying from his head under the helmet. His transformation complete, he simply stood there, letting me look at him.

I didn't scream, for which I am profoundly proud. I didn't pass out, or start gibbering at him either. I just sat on my bed and took in this giant standing in my dorm room, his helmeted head somehow only grazing the ceiling. I was in a state of shock, I suppose. After several incredibly long minutes, I was shocked to hear my voice, which sounded completely normal to my ears, say, "You look like an extra from "Erik the Viking", man."

Heimdall threw back his head and laughed. It seemed like it shook the whole dorm, and I could faintly hear someone down the hall way scream "What the fuck was *that?!?*" Heimdall looked at me sheepishly. When he spoke, his voice was barely above a whisper, but it still reverberated off the walls of my room, shaking the bottles of beer on my desk. "I'm going to change back now. I can't speak in a normal tone in this form, because I might cause the building to fall in."

I was all for that. "By all means, please change back. As a matter of fact, feel free to change back somewhere other than here. This is too weird for me to deal with. I need a nap."

He grinned at me, shrinking back into his normal clothing and size. "I would imagine a nap would be something you might want at this moment, Alex, but I'm afraid you're not going to be able to get one just yet. We have places we need to be, and things we need to do."

"Uh-uh, not this kid", I told him. "I'm not going anywhere with you. I think I may be having a bit of a mental breakdown or something. This isn't happening. You're not really here, and I'm just drunk."

He nodded again. "I understand this is a bit much for you. Let me ask you a question. What language are we speaking?"

The question took me off guard. This guy had a real talent for derailing my thought process. I shook my head. "English. We're speaking English. Besides a few Russian phrases, English is the only language I speak. I failed French in high school." But even as I said this, I realized that while I could understand everything he and I were saying, it didn't sound quite right. The words themselves were correct, but they didn't sound like the English I had grown up learning. Heimdall continued grinning. He said, "Repeat this after me: 'Glory is in battle.'"

I did as he asked, and was absolutely floored at the words coming out of my mouth. "Í bardaga er dýrð." I looked at him, mute with shock. I knew that I had said what he had said, but he was right, neither of us had said it in English. I sat there gaping like a landed catfish until I could stammer out, "What the *fuck* is going on?"

The smile never left his face. "We're speaking Old Norse. Now, for someone that can't pass a French class, how is it you're fluent in Old Norse?"

I had no answer to that, so I just sat there staring at him.

Finally, I spoke. "You aren't screwing around with me, are you? This isn't some sort of trick, something to just mess with my head, is it?"

His smile disappeared. "No, little brother, it's not. I wish that it were. I hate to involve you in any of this, but it must be done, for your safety and that of your family."

Although the whole situation still felt unreal to me, there was a part of me that not only accepted what this man was saying was true, but rejoiced in it. Taking a breath, I told him, "I think you better start at the beginning, big guy. I need some answers here. What the hell is going on?"

Sitting back down in my easy chair, Heimdall began

his tale.

Chapter Three

"This story starts over a thousand years ago", he said. "The world was much different than the one you live in. Odin, the Allfather, was on one of his many trips to Midgard to mix freely with the race of man, as was his habit. He came upon a small village of the *Rus*, on the River Volga. It is the place you now call Russia. It was settled by Norsemen that had spread their trade routes all over the known world and in some cases, beyond. Odin moved among man in the guise of an old traveler, seeing what men did and how they lived. In this small village, he stopped for the night at the home of a moderately wealthy family of Norsemen and asked for shelter for the night. He as welcomed in, as was the custom of all the Norse, and given food and drink, as well as a place to stay the night.

"The daughter of the man of the house was a girl of exceptional beauty. She was kind to the old traveler, and made sure he was comfortable. She and Odin stayed up late into the night, talking of many things. Odin was taken in by her beauty and fell in thrall to her. Revealing himself in his true form, he asked that she be his for just one night. The girl, overcoming her shock, was honored to be desired by the Allfather, and readily agreed.

"Now, I don't want you getting the idea that Odin just went from place to place debauching young girls. That was more along Zeus' line. Odin has a beautiful wife, Frigg, whom he loves dearly. She was hurt and upset by Odin's affair with this mortal girl, but she forgave him for it. The girl's name was Sygny, and she was as fair as a summer day. They spent only the one night together, the Allfather casting a spell over the house that all would remain asleep and give them privacy.

"The next morning Odin, now back in his guise of an old traveler, left the home of the *Rus* and went back to Asgard to his hall. Although he never returned to the girl or her family, he kept a watchful eye on them, and granted them favor when he could. After a few months, it was apparent that Sygny was with child. Her father was furious and gave all the village to know that his daughter had been whoring herself. Sygny swore on all the gods that she had known the touch of only one man, and that he was a god. Her father beat her when she told of her night with the Allfather. And although Odin had sworn to Frigg that he would never again see the girl, he refused to stand by and see her mistreated in that manner."

"So, he sent me to the tiny village of the *Rus*. There, I told the father and all the villagers the truth of the girl's words. She carried within her the son of Odin, and should be given all honors due her. The villagers grew pale as I spoke, and the girl's father apologized profusely for his actions. When I left the village, Sygny and her family were elevated to the rulers of the village. In the fullness of time, the village grew to become the city of Novgorod. Sygny's family remained in power there for generations, each firstborn son of the female line taking the mantle of power.

"This, like all things, faded with time, and the family became just one more family among thousands of others. Governments came and went, but Sygny's family line remained. From mother to son, each generation spreading farther and farther into the world. And all the while, the Allfather kept his eye on his mortal family, giving help when he could.

"Flash forward to the modern age, and the terrible war that came to Russia at the hands of the Germans in the 1940's. Millions perished. For a time, it seemed that the human line of Odin would forever be lost. However, the Allfather was able to shield some of his mortal sons and daughters from the horrors of war, and move them to safety after the fighting had ended.

Here, Heimdall stopped, and gave me a long and penetrating stare. "It was your mother's parents that came to this new world from the ashes of the old. They moved here and they thrived. They were no longer the powerful family they had once been, but the Allfather thought it better that they live normal, anonymous lives here. In this manner, they would be safe from any enemies that might try to harm them.

"That is why you, Alexei, are who and what you are. Your size and strength mark you. You look nothing like your parents, because the blood that flows within your veins is that of a god. You are the direct descendent of Sygny and the Allfather."

I had been trying to take all this in stride, but now my reserve broke. "Are you trying to tell me that my great-great-great-great-great-great-great-great grandfather was Odin???"

He smiled. "Not exactly. It doesn't quite work like that. While there are many human generations separating you from the Allfather, he is not your grandfather. He is your father, the same as your mortal father. The intervening years do not change what you are. The blood of the Allfather runs through your veins without any dilution. Your mortal father gave your mother the seed that created you, but by blood, you are Odin's son entire. Just as I am."

I shook my head. "Okay, that explains the 'little brother' comments, I suppose. But even if I accept all this, which I'm not saying that I *do*, but even if I did, what difference would it make, and why are you here?"

Heimdall reached into the pocket of his pea coat and withdrew a many-folded newspaper, smudged and grimy. He tossed it towards me. I caught it reflexively, and looked at it. It was a national paper from a month prior. I looked at it, and then back up at Heimdall in confusion. "What am I looking for?"

He nodded toward the front page. "The story below the fold."

I looked at the picture accompanying the text. There were huge billowing clouds of smoke and fire rising up from a huge hole in the ground. Rescue teams and firemen rushed about, attempting to put out the blaze. The caption read "Massive underground explosion kills 48 in Norway". I scanned the story. It seemed that there had been a mine explosion that had rocked the countryside. There were no survivors reported. I looked back up at Heimdall, my eyebrows raised in question.

He leaned back again, his eyes on the ceiling. "What do you know about Loki?" he asked.

I thought for a moment, trying to dredge up that old report. "He was a sworn blood-brother to Odin, and he was called the 'Trickster' because of all the problems he caused the gods, right?"

Heimdall nodded. "Yes, but 'problems' are a bit of an understatement. Loki's sense of humor was always dark, but after the death of Balder, he became more and more evil. It was foretold by the Norns that Loki would be instrumental in bringing about Ragnarok."

"What are the Norns, and who is Balder?" I asked.

"You would call the Norns the Fates. They decree the length of all life. They know everything that has ever happened, or ever will. Even Odin is powerless to change their decrees. He has spent millennia trying to extract from them the date of Ragnarok, but to no avail. Balder is one of the gods, the most handsome of us all and the god of all things beautiful. Upon his birth, his mother made all things promise to never bring him harm. Only one thing was missed, a tiny mistletoe plant, something so small and innocent that no thought was given that it might harm Balder. The gods amused themselves by throwing axes and spears at him, and shooting him with arrows. None of these things hurt him at all. But Loki brought, Höd, Balder's blind brother, a dart made of mistletoe. Not knowing what he was throwing, Höd threw the dart and killed Balder. Höd, in his grief, killed himself." Heimdall stopped speaking and shook his head, as if to clear it. "Enough history. Something has happened that has changed everything"

"Wait a minute", I interrupted. "Are you honestly telling me that all the Christians, Jews, Muslims, Buddhists, hell, *all* the other religions have got it all wrong? How can that be? Judaism is older than the Norse gods. How can the other religions be wrong when they pre-date this one?"

He sighed. "It's a very long story, and hard for a mortal mind to fathom, but I'll give you the Reader's Digest version of things. The gods, and I mean *all* of the gods, of *every* people, are the physical manifestation of man's thought, his faith. In essence, man creates us with his worship. Jesus walked the earth, just as it is written in the Bible. But he only became a god when man decided it was so. The same for Zeus, Buddha, Odin…all of the gods. Once man has imagined us and begun his worship, we appear. And through man's worship, we are given the powers he attributes to us."

He was right; this mortal mind was having a very difficult time fathoming what he was saying. "Are you telling me that the gods exist because we *invent* them???"

He smiled wearily. "Yes, in a matter of speaking. You see, we are all interconnected in the Universe. Your mathematicians and scientists are not far from the truth of things. Every atom has a direct effect on every other atom. It's far too complex to explain, but in essence, you are correct. Man brings the gods into existence, not the other way around."

I thought for moment. "So, before man recognized you as a god, what were you?"

"I was nothing. I did not exist. I sprang into existence knowing everything that man said I should know, and having all the powers that man thought I should have. It is the same for all the other gods, as well. I remember nothing from before the time I was worshipped as a god. Myself, I believe that there is something else behind all of this, an ultimate god, the 'God of Gods', if you wish, that controls everything. However, I have never seen this creator. I suspect he or she or it is there, but I cannot say that I can prove it. I merely have faith that it exists."

I couldn't help myself. I laughed out loud. Heimdall looked at me quizzically. "It's just ironic to me that a god has to make a leap of faith regarding another god", I told him.

He smiled and nodded. "Yes, it is ironic. However, because I am, because I exist and wield the power that I do, I can only imagine that there must be a god far more powerful than I to have brought us *all* into existence. But we're digressing. Back to Loki. Is there anything else you remember about him?"

I shook my head. "Not really. I just remember that he was kind of a bastard. I know that he was punished somehow, but I can't remember how."

Heimdall nodded towards the paper in my hands. "Yes, he was punished. Gravely. The story you read there relates to that punishment. After the death of Balder, the Aesir decided that Loki was to be fettered underground until the coming of Ragnarok. He was tied to a boulder deep within the earth with his son Narvi's entrails. A serpent drips venom onto his face for all time. His wife Sigyn holds a cup to catch the venom, but when she must empty it, he thrashes about in pain, thus causing earthquakes."

I gave him a pained look. "You tied him to a rock with his son's guts and let a snake drip venom on him? You guys are a little hardcore, aren't you?"

He looked at me, his eyes flashing angrily. "You forget that Loki is the cause of my brother's death, and untold pain and misery, both in Midgard *and* in Asgard. He deserved his punishment."

I shrugged. "If you say so. But what does this", I held up the paper, "have to do with that?"

"Workers in that mine were drilling and blasting into the earth in search of ores. In their greed, they unwittingly freed Loki from his bondage. His wrath was terrible. He destroyed everything in that mine, killing the men working within it. He was set loose on Midgard, and he is at large here still."

A faint memory of that old report surfaced. "Loki is supposed to help bring Ragnarok about, right? Is that what this is all about? Are we about to see the end of days, or something?"

Heimdall looked at the floor between his feet. "Do you keep up with world events?"

"I try to. I mean, it's not exactly on the top of my to-do list, but I try to watch the news every couple of days. Why?"

"Have you noticed anything unusual lately?"

I thought about it. The news from around the world had been pretty busy lately. "Well", I said, "there's been a series of clashes in North Africa lately. Egypt, Tunisia, Libya, all of the people of those countries have overthrown their governments. Also, for some reason, France and Germany are acting awfully weird towards each other. Something about a boundary line. Both countries are claiming to own the land in question, and it's making things a little tense in Europe right now. My World Civ. professor was joking that it looked like we were about to get involved with another European war for the third time in a century."

He nodded. "Yes, all that and more. The countries of this planet are slowly heading for conflict. It will begin with small things, border disputes, civil unrest, and things like that. However, before it is done, all the world will be involved in a truly world-wide conflict. Brother will kill brother, father will kill son… it will be the end of all things."

I could feel my insides turn to jelly. My voice barely above a whisper, I said, "You're telling me that Armageddon is coming. That the world is going to end. Jesus Christ."

He gave me a level stare. "No, I am telling you all the

things that *may* be, not all the things that *will* be."

I was at a loss. "But you said that the, what did you call them… the Norns had decreed that Ragnarok was inevitable, that Loki was going to fuck everything up. Even Odin couldn't change it, you said."

He nodded again, his face set in grim lines. "Yes, this is true. However, as I said before, something has changed. We Aesir were called to the Well of the Norns to hear what they had to say. They were flustered, even frightened. This alone was enough to turn our legs weak. The Norns are *never* frightened. They spoke to us, saying that Loki's freedom was not supposed to happen yet. They would not tell us when Ragnarok was to come; only that it was *not* supposed to come now. Something has upset the entire universe. Loki's freedom has changed the fate of all creatures, both man and god alike."

I lay back on the bed, staring at the ceiling. This was just too much for me to take in. Just a few hours ago, I had been just one more struggling student trying to make ends meet in college, and now I was dealing with the fact that my father was an ancient god, and that the end of time was upon us. And I thought my Sociology test was going to be hard. Finally, I got up onto my elbows and looked at Heimdall.

"Okay, thanks for the great revelation. I'm the son of a god, and I've only got a little while to live. You're just chock full of great news, bro."

He laughed. "You're not listening. These things don't have to come to pass. If there was nothing to be done about it, I wouldn't be here telling you all this. What would have been the point? 'Hey, there little brother, you're a demi-god, and you're screwed!' That makes no sense. I came to you so we can stop this from happening."

"How? I mean, if you guys could catch Loki once, you can do it again, right? I'd just kill his ass, if I were you. That way Ragnarok couldn't ever happen in the first place."

Heimdall shook his head in disgust. "You *still* aren't listening. We are at the mercy of the Norns. Their word is law. We cannot kill Loki. Ragnarok *will* happen. Just not right now. We have to stop Loki, and fetter him again in the earth until the proper time."

My head was reeling. All I wanted to do was get some sleep. "Well, fine, catch him and tie his ass back up in a hole. I'm all for it. None of this has dick-all to do with me. Why are you here?"

"You are a singularity. You possess half the blood of the Allfather. You and you alone can pass over Bifrost and into Asgard as a mortal. No other mortal can do so unless they are dead.'

Lucky me, I thought.

"Over the millennia, Loki has lost much of his power. He cannot cross Bifrost anymore, either. And if he cannot cross Bifrost, he cannot enter Asgard. Ragnarok cannot occur."

"Well", I said, "where's the problem with that? Sounds to me like you guys are sitting pretty. If he can't get in, Ragnarok is on permanent hiatus, and you guys aren't disobeying the Norns. Problem solved."

He smiled at me in a way that chilled my heart. "Oh yes", he said, "Problem solved, indeed. There's just one small problem with that. *You.* The singularity. *You* can cross between the worlds because of who you are. Things were at a stalemate before Loki learned of your existence. Now he knows who and what you are. He can kill you and absorb your power. Then, he *can* cross Bifrost. Follow me now, little brother?"

I could feel my teeth trying to chatter. "How did he find out about me?"

"I have no idea. No one does. He has always been cunning. How he found out is irrelevant, anyway. He knows about you, little brother. He will be coming for you soon, if he isn't already on his way. And if he finds you here in this squalid dorm room reading your Sociology text, just what do you plan to do about it? Politely ask him to leave? That didn't work with me, and I'm on *your* side. He would laugh at you and eat your still-beating heart before your eyes."

I laughed weakly. "Well, if he eats my heart before my eyes, at least I'll be able to see him do it. Makes more sense that way. If he ate my eyes first, I wouldn't be able to see anything."

Heimdall smiled. "Gallows humor. I like it. Now, are you coming with me, or am I going to have to knock you unconscious and drag you?"

"Easy, big guy. Go with you where?"

"Home, of course. To Asgard. Your father would very much like to meet you."

Chapter Four

In a shallow, dank cave on a thickly wooded hillside, Loki sat by a small fire. He gazed into the flames and rocked gently back and forth. His eyes, one green and one red, flared with firelight. They held nothing but pure madness and horrifying glee.

His face was a roadmap of scar tissue. He looked like a model of Frankenstein's monster fashioned by a cruelly talented child. Fissures of flesh rose among the craters, a ruination of what once had been a handsome face. He muttered under his breath constantly, a low maddening sound. From the far corner of the cave came a rustling of cloth, and Loki's faithful wife came towards him with a plate of bread and cheese.

"Will you not take some food, my husband?" asked Sigyn.

Loki did not turn from the fire. From the corner of his twisted mouth he spat, "I will eat *nothing*, woman, *nothing* until I eat from the table of the Aesir. Then I will glut myself of their fare and dance in their blood. Leave me be."

Sigyn recoiled. She turned back to her pallet in the back of the cave and lay down, covering herself with a fur. She could not understand what was happening. For millennia, she had been faithfully by his side, keeping him from pain. Since his freedom, he had been nothing short of vile towards her, and she could not understand what she had done to deserve such treatment. Finally, she found the courage and asked him why he treated her so.

Loki's head whipped around like a striking serpent. His mad gaze fell upon her on her pallet, and she whimpered and pulled her fur over her face. His voice dripped sarcastic hatred when he spoke. "Why do I treat you so?" he mimicked in a falsetto. "Why do I treat you so? Look at my face, woman!" She refused to lower the fur. "LOOK AT ME!" he bellowed. She lowered the fur until her eyes were showing. Tears sparkled in them as she looked into the face of her husband.

"Why do I treat you so? Why should I not? Look upon this face and see what you have done! I should tear you limb from limb and toss them to the winds, that is what I should do! And you dare ask why I treat you so!"

Sigyn was utterly confused. "But my husband", she replied weakly, her voice thick with tears, "It was I that kept the serpent from spilling its venom on you. Yes, it hurt you and scarred you, but only when I had to empty the cup! What was I to do? I had to empty the cup, did I not?"

Loki's eyes bulged out of his face, his visage contorted with fury. "Did you never think to get TWO cups, you ignorant whore??? One to fill and another to hold in place whilst you emptied the FIRST???"

Sigyn wept openly now. "But, my Lord, you never told me to do such a thing! I would have done so immediately had you but said the word!"

Loki fairly went mad with fury. He danced in place, flinging his arms around him like a whirlwind. "I??? I should have thought of it??? Did you not notice that I was in AGONY, gods damn you??? Must I think of EVERYTHING???"

Sigyn covered her face again and shuddered as sobs wracked her body. Loki stood over her for a moment longer, panting with exertion, and then all the rage fell from his face like a window blind. His eyes turned again to the fire, and he returned to his place in front of it, staring into its depths. He began mumbling again, his voice an insane monotone. It was counter pointed by piteous sobs from his wife. Loki took no notice of her, but remained as he was throughout the night.

As the sun began to creep into the eastern sky, he finally stood. Casting a hate-filled look towards his wife, he said, "Are you coming with me, you useless cow, or are you going to spend the day weeping in your corner? I've much to do, and time grows short. Come or stay, it means little to me." With that, he turned and left the cave, making his way down the hillside. Sigyn gathered up their meager belongings and hurried after him. She called for him to wait for her several times, but he ignored her completely.

As he walked briskly down the hill and toward the city below, he continued his mumbling. It was only two words, spoken over and over. "Alexei Addison…Alexei Addison…Alexei Addison…Alexei Addison…" He moved rapidly. The time to end this farce was nearing. He would not have his glory stolen again.

Sigyn hurried along behind him, struggling with her load, tears rolling freely down her beautiful face.

Chapter Five

Heimdall and I stood in the center of the U.K.
football stadium. It was almost four in the morning, and
I had never been so tired in all my life. He wouldn't tell
me why we were here, only that I needed to gather my
clothing. "Find something warm" had been his only
instruction.

So here I stood, at the fifty yard line of the football
field, wearing my warmest coat and a pair of heavy
leather gloves. I had changed my wet pants for a clean
pair, and put on new socks and my old hiking boots. I
glanced over at Heimdall, still not able to truly believe
what was happening to me. He stood, silent and still,
looking up into the night sky.

After we had stood that way for almost an hour, my
patience finally gave way. "What the fuck are we doing
here, besides catching a really nasty case of pneumonia?"
I asked sarcastically. He merely turned his head and
gave me a look that shut me up quickly. "Fine, okay,
whatever", I mumbled under my breath.

After what seemed an eternity, he pointed to the sky.

"There, do you see it?" he asked.

I looked to where he was pointing, but couldn't see anything but the dimming stars as the sun began to lighten the sky. "See what?" I asked.

"Just keep looking. You'll see it. Your eyes aren't quite what mine are."

So I continued to stare at the patch of sky he had indicated. I was beginning to think he was screwing with me when I noticed that the stars in that patch of sky had taken on a blurry cast. Soon, colors began to swirl from them. It was like looking at the Aurora Borealis, only confined to one small part of the sky. It snaked its way down from the stars until it stopped at our feet. It was the most beautiful thing I had ever seen. All the colors of the spectrum played back and forth across it.

His voice full of pride, Heimdall said, "Bifrost, the Rainbow Bridge."

I was too full of wonder to answer.

He began to walk towards it. With a jolt, I snapped out of my reverie and followed him. I wasn't sure what to expect. Was he going to simply start walking up this thing into the sky? I was suddenly beset by doubts. Could I really follow him? It was one thing to hear him tell me that I was the son of Odin so casually, but quite another to think that I could defy all the laws of physics and gravity itself and simply walk into the sky.

To my relief, he did not start walking up towards the stars. Instead, he stood inside the prism of color and turned to look at me. "Coming?" he asked. I nodded, and stepped tentatively towards the rainbow. I stopped just short of it, he on the inside and me on the out. I reached out to touch the shimmering colors when I heard him give an exasperated snort. His huge hand reached out through the haze of color and grabbed me by the front of my coat. Before I could voice my indignation, I found myself standing with him inside the rainbow.

I can't adequately describe what it looked like from the inside. As I looked through the colors that played themselves across what looked like a glass wall, I could see the football field on the other side. It looked like an old, sepia-toned picture. I turned to Heimdall and sucked in a surprised breath. Inside the rainbow, he looked his normal self. Gone was the pea coat and jeans. He was attired as he had been in my dorm room, his armor and helmet reflecting back the full spectrum of color.

To my surprise, I no longer needed to look up at him. In fact, he was almost the same height as I was. I looked down at myself and was shocked yet again. My clothes, bought from a big and tall shop so they would fit me well, now appeared to be several sizes too small. My coat came halfway up my forearms, and my pants stopped several inches above my ankles. My feet felt cramped in my boots, and they looked like they were threatening to burst open at the seams. My t-shirt was chokingly tight around my neck. I reached up with one hand and tugged at the collar, which gave way with a ripping noise. The buckle of my belt and the waistband of my jeans burst simultaneously, the button of my jeans shooting back out of the rainbow and on to the brown grass of the football field.

I looked at Heimdall with a stupid expression stamped on my face. He laughed uproariously. I reached up to push my hair out of my eyes, hair that had grown a full foot or more in an instant, when I caught sight of my high school ring. It was stretched, the metal as thin as paper in places. My fingers were three times as big as they had been. I was pulling a David Banner. If it weren't for the vast array of colors, I would have feared I was turning green.

"What the *fuck* is happening to me?" I demanded. My voice, already a deep bass, now sounded like the growl of a wolf on steroids and crystal meth.

Heimdall had managed to control himself, and was now only chuckling a little. Between giggles, he explained what was going on.

"You look as you truly are now", he said, tears running down his face from his mirth. "This is your true image. Did you truly think that a son of the Allfather would be as puny as you were?"

"Puny?!?" I yelled. "What do you mean, 'puny'? I'm six-seven, dammit! I'm a giant!"

He chuckled a bit more. "Maybe in the world of Man you're a giant, but here, six-seven is about the size of our smaller women folk." He gave me an evil grin.

I was getting pissed. "All right, fine, you had your little joke. Now what the hell am I going to do? Don't think that I'm going to show up in front a bunch of gods and goddesses looking like this, dammit."

He kept grinning, but waved his hand over my body. The constricting bands of my clothing eased instantly. I looked down at myself and was floored once again by what I saw. I was dressed much like Heimdall, in leather pants and tunic. Heavy plates of armor and chain mail hung from my shoulders, and I had bracers similar to his, but with a different design set into them. My coat had transformed into what appeared to be a bear fur. I was thankful of that, because it was cold inside the rainbow.

I looked down at my waist and saw that there was a huge sword and axe hanging there. I pulled the sword out of the scabbard. It was fully six feet long and looked like it would have weighted a hundred pounds, easy. I would have had a hard time holding it up normally, but now I could swing it as easily as I could a baseball bat. I admired it for a few moments and then slid it back home. I looked up to find Heimdall looking at me with amusement.

"What?" I asked, defensively.

"Nothing", he replied. "You just look better now, that's all. You look more natural."

"Right", I said. "Natural. I look like Andre the Giant, and I'm armed to the damn teeth. Sure. Natural."

He gave me his wicked little grin again and clapped me on the shoulder. "Come on, little brother. We've got some ground to cover Oh, and by the way, you should tone down your language. The Allfather doesn't care for profanity."

He turned and started off. I shook my head. "Great.

The Allfather of the Vikings doesn't care for profanity. What's next, etiquette lessons from Miss Manners?"

"I heard that", Heimdall said over his shoulder as he walked towards Bifrost. Although from the outside, the bottom of the rainbow had appeared to be about ten feet square; as he moved off I could see that it seemed to go on forever. I took a few long strides to catch up and looked around. The farther we moved from the football field, the more it seemed like we were walking in a multi-colored tunnel.

"Is this how you travel back and forth?" I asked.

He nodded. "Yes. Although sometimes I ride my chariot. I figured we would walk, so you could acclimate yourself a little. Loki can't harm you here, and it gives you some time to ready yourself for Asgard. You'll be seeing it through mortal eyes, remember. That's not something any man has done."

At the mention of Loki, I grew immediately concerned. I grabbed Heimdall by the shoulder and said, "My parents! Shit, my *grandparents*! Loki might not be able to hurt *me*, but what's to stop him from going after *them*? We've got to go back!"

Heimdall shook his head patiently. "I told you I wouldn't let anything happen to your family, and I meant it. They are safe, I assure you."

"Safe how?" I asked suspiciously.

He rolled his eyes. "Your family is in a sort of suspended animation. They are awake, but they have been pulled out of the stream of time. They are in a sort of in-between place, halfway between Midgard and Asgard. They think it's simply the evening. They're watching TV, relaxing. They're in a sort of timeless bubble. And guarding that bubble are two hundred hand-picked Einherjar, chosen by Odin himself. Trust me, *I* wouldn't want to mess with these particular Einherjar, and I could defeat just about anyone. He won't bother your family. Besides, once he realizes you are in Asgard, it would do him no good to try. You're completely out of the mortal world now, and beyond his influence."

"What are Einherjar?" I asked, still not certain about my family's safety.

He rolled his eyes again. "Honestly, you should show a bit more interest in your family history, you know that? The Einherjar are the slain heroes, picked by the Valkyries to live in Valhalla until Ragnarok. Only the bravest and the best warriors get that honor. Two hundred of them could hold off every Marine on your world, and still have time to play a few hands of cards. Trust me; your family is well protected. Once we've met with the Allfather, you will be able to look in on them, I'm sure."

I wasn't totally convinced, but then again, I wasn't totally convinced I hadn't bashed my head against the staircase in my dorm and wasn't dreaming all this. I decided to let it go for now. Instead, I took in the sights.

It was cold, as I mentioned, and the ground was covered in snow and ice. It seemed more like we were on a wooded path than a tunnel now. Everything was lit by the spectrum, lights playing back and forth across the sky. It was beautiful and silent. Far in the distance, I could see a mountain that the path climbed. At the summit, I could just make out huge buildings, firelight playing through the windows. We were still far off, so I could only imagine how large the buildings truly were. To pass the time, I questioned Heimdall about his world.

He told me of the gods, and what each was responsible for. Every god had a job, a specific thing that he or she was directly responsible for tending. I was surprised to learn that Thor, the most famous of the gods in my world, was actually quite stupid. Heimdall warned me that saying so in his presence was a very bad idea. I found myself asking questions about Odin. This was my father, in a manner of speaking. I couldn't quite grasp the concept that he was my actual father. That honor belonged to my dad, and always would. But it was Odin's blood in my veins, and it was about him I was most curious.

Heimdall told me about how Odin was a friend of Man, and always had been. It was Odin that had traded one of his eyes for a single drink from the Well of Knowledge guarded by Mimir, and he had shared that knowledge with Man. It was Odin that had hung from Yggdrasill, the World Tree, for nine nights, pierced by a spear, to gain the knowledge of the Runes, which he shared with Man. He hung there for nine nights, died, and was reborn.

"Wait a minute!" I shouted. "He hung from a tree, was pierced by a spear, died, and then came back to life? That's just what happened to Jesus!"

Heimdall smiled. "Yes, I know. Religion isn't always what you think it is little brother. You must remember that all religion is passed along by men. Whether they pass it down in song or story, or write it in books, it is all done by man, and man is fallible. Things can get garbled, mistranslated. Men are often tempted to add to or take from religious writings that which they feel should be there, or that which they feel does not belong.

Purists, those that will read a religious tract and take it word-for-word as literal truth, are forever doomed to be in the darkness… the absence of the light of truth. Religion is a guide, nothing more. Each man is born knowing what is right from what is wrong. From the cradle, man is given the knowledge of true right and wrong. To murder the innocent, this is wrong. You didn't need anyone to teach you this, any more than you needed to be taught that it was wrong to steal what another possessed. Many think these things need to be taught, that they are a learned response, but this is wrong. You knew these things from your earliest memories."

I laughed. "I'm being given a lesson in morality from one of the gods of the most violent groups of people in history."

Heimdall laughed right back. "Yes, they lived in a violent time, and they behaved accordingly. However, they did not do things that were dishonorable lightly, for they knew that judgment would fall upon them if they did."

"Heimdall, my man, you are one weird dude."

He smiled sadly. "I am what man made me."

That struck home. Although the sense of disassociation was still strong, the stoic grief of the individual beside me could not be ignored. On impulse, I placed my hand on his shoulder.

"You really don't like being a god, do you?"

He seemed surprised by the question. His brow furrowed in thought. We walked on in silence for a long time before he finally spoke again.

"I don't know if it's a matter of liking or not liking what I am. I didn't ask to be what I am, any more than you did. However, the fact is this: I was brought into being by a race of man that decided my fate without giving me a chance to even consult them about it. At least with the Christians, their belief system revolves around God being the one to decide when the time has come to end everything. And even at that, the world will be a Heaven afterwards. The Norsemen believed much the same thing. After Ragnarok, there will be two humans left, and theirs will be a world of plenty, where peace and love will reign forever." He paused for a moment, thinking.

"Well, that's not so bad then, is it?" I asked. "After Ragnarok, you can look forward to an eternity of paradise."

He looked at me quickly, anger rising in his eyes. When he saw my confusion, his eyes cleared, and he smiled at me. "I forget you aren't very well versed in the Norse belief system. After Ragnarok, I will be dead, never to return. Odin will be dead. Thor, Freyr, Tyr…

all will be dead. Surt will fling fire from his sword, engulfing the nine worlds. Everything will die, save Lif and Lifthrasir, the man and woman that will survive by hiding deep within Yggdrasill. It is their children that will inherit this paradise you speak of. Of the gods, some of Thor's sons will live on, and Balder and Höd will return from the dead. Honir will be there, as will the sons of Vili and Ve. These remaining gods will make up the new Aesir. But for those of us that are doomed... our lives will end, and there will be no afterlife."

Now it was my turn to be silent for a time. Finally, I said, "Heimdall, you know that you're going to die during Ragnarok? I mean, are you sure?"

He smiled. "Yes, Alex, I'm sure. I even know who is going to kill me. Of course, I'm going to kill him as well, so at least there's that."

"You already know who's going to kill you? What the fuck? Sorry about the 'fuck'. It's going to take me a while to get used to not saying that. Who kills you? Who is it?"

Heimdall looked off into the distance at the massive buildings atop the mountain. "Loki, of course. Loki and I are destined to kill one another."

Chapter Six

An eternity and a heartbeat away, Loki stood in the center of what was left of Alex's dorm room. His fury was spent, and the room bore evidence of it. Smoke curled from the floor, the walls, and the furniture. Nothing remained in one piece. Alex's clothing was shredded into slim, gauzy strips. His textbooks were burnt relics. The glass from his window wasn't broken; it had been rendered into a fine power. Dimly, in the hallway, a smoke alarm blared. Sigyn cowered in the corner of the room, whimpering.

Loki spun on his heel and walked back towards the door to the room. It was barely hanging, one hinge precariously holding it upright. He stalked into the hallway, where the smoke was much thicker. He had lost much of his power, but the ability to destroy with his will alone was still intact, if less effective than it once was. He began to make his way down the wreckage of the hallway, stepping over the smoldering body of a campus police officer. The man's face was gone, and a blackened skull grinned up at Loki as he passed.

Luckily for the students that resided in the dorm, the majority had been in their first class of the day when Loki had arrived at the campus of the University of Kentucky. The few that didn't have an early class or those that simply skipped class that morning were not so fortunate. Their twisted and mangled bodies lay sprawled, their faces contorted in death. There were about thirty bodies in all. One of these still hung on to life by a thread.

His name was Isaac Macintyre. He was a nineteen year old freshman from a small town on the Kentucky-Tennessee border. His mother had asked him repeatedly to go to the University of Tennessee, so he would be closer to home, but Isaac had refused, wanting nothing more than to finally be free of his overbearing mother. His desire for freedom was to cost him his life.

Loki walked by the room where Isaac lay on the floor, weeping and trying to hold his intestines in. A piece of mirror had spun across his room during the height of Loki's rage and neatly disemboweled him. Isaac heard someone walking down the smoke-filled hallway and cried out for help.

He should have remained silent.

Loki walked into Isaac's room and stood in the doorway, staring down at him. Isaac took one look into the destroyed face and the two-tone eyes full of mirthful madness and forgot all about the ropes of intestines lying in his lap. He began to scoot backward, his hands and buttocks the only things touching the floor. He bumped into the wall and could go no further. *I'm having a nightmare*, he thought feverishly. *This is just some sort of*

nightmare. I shouldn't have smoked that pot with James last
night. I bet it was laced with something.

Loki strode into the room and stood over Isaac,
looking down at him with a cheerful smile on his face.

"Hi, there!"

Isaac squeezed his eyes shut, whipping his head from
side to side in negation. Loki was pressed for time, so
he did the one thing he knew would get Isaac's
attention: He stepped on Isaac's testicles and twisted his
heel.

Isaac Macintyre screamed so loudly that blood
welled up in the back of his throat in large beads. His
eyes sprang open like exploding landmines. His vision
went red and all the world was pain. Pain unlike
anything he could have ever imagined. No one could
really feel this kind of pain; it was a thing of myth, of
horror stories told around a campfire. It was in him, the
pain was in him, he was being eaten from the inside out
by some miserable creature of fangs and claws. Oh, it
was in him, it was in him, it was right *inside* him.

Certain that he had Isaac's undivided attention, Loki
took his booted heel off of the mangled testicle on the
floor. He hunkered down so that his face was level with
Isaac's. The smile never left its place. Loki positively
radiated cheer and mirth. Having gotten Isaac's
attention, he tried again.

"Hi, there!"

Isaac swallowed a lump of blood and bile. This
horror seemed to need a response, so Isaac gave it the

only one he could think of.

"H-h-h-hello…"

Loki beamed at him. Here was some progress! "Say, my good fellow, would you by any chance be familiar with the young man that lives in room 421? Strapping young man, goes by the name of Alex Addison?"

Isaac watched as the color leaked out of the room. Blackness edged his vision. *Oh, thank you, Jesus! I'm passing out!* From the corner of his eyes, through the darkness, he saw a look and anger surge across the madman's face. With great deliberation, the man reached over and picked up an ink pen from the desk beside him. Looking Isaac in the eyes, he raised it above his head and slammed it down, pinning Isaac's swollen and bloody testicle to the floor.

The blessing of unconsciousness was ripped from him like a blanket on a cold morning. He tried to scream again, but could make only a high tea kettle sound. Blood and slime flew from his mouth. The blackness receded instantly. Isaac slammed his head against the wall behind him over and over.

Loki bent over and whispered gently into Isaac's ear. "Would you like the pain to stop?"

Yes, mouthed Isaac, still unable to speak. Loki nodded. "All right then. Here's what I'll do for you. I'll take your pain away, and you will answer my questions. You'll answer them promptly and you'll answer them honestly. Should you fail to do either of these things, I will send the pain back into you, but I think I'll magnify it by about ten times. How does that sound? Have we a deal?"

Isaac nodded wildly. Anything to take this agony away. Loki reached out and brushed the side of Isaac's face gently, like a mother cooling a fevered child's brow.

The pain faded instantly. Isaac looked in mute wonder into the eyes of the man that had taken his pain away. One green eye, one red, they danced and twirled with crazed inner light.

Loki nodded. "There, now. That's better, isn't it?"

Isaac nodded again, still unable to find his voice.

"All right. Now, as I was saying, are you familiar with the young man in room 421? Young Master Addison?"

Isaac nodded, then licked his lips and said in a weak voice he didn't recognize as his own, "Yeah, I know Alex. He's a big guy. Really tall and muscular. He used to play football."

Loki clapped his hands in delight. "Wonderful! Football, you say! That is just superb! An athlete! Of course, he would be! Now, my good man, whatever might your name be?"

"Isaac... Isaac M-M-Macintyre, sir."

"*Sir*, no less! What a well-mannered young man you are! Did you learn such impeccable manners from your mother and father, dear boy?"

"My m-mother, sir. My dad d-d-died when I was little."

Loki's face turned into a horrid parody of grief. "Died when you were little? How very terrible for you! You must have been devastated! So, it was your mother that has forged such a fine specimen of well-mannered youth, then?"

"Y-y-yes, sir."

"Grand! Just grand! Well, tell me, young Isaac, have you by chance seen Alex Addison this fine day?"

Isaac shook his head. "No, sir. I haven't s-s-seen him since last night."

Loki's countenance darkened. "Oh, that is truly a sad thing for you. I'm afraid I cannot use you if you have no information about Alex. A pity, really. I was just beginning to think you and I were going to be great friends." Loki reached down towards the ink pen skewering Isaac's testicle to the floor. The effect was galvanizing. Isaac's stutter disappeared, and he found strength to speak surge through his torn body.

"NO!!! No, please!!! I saw him last night! I saw him in the hallway, going to his room with a huge fucking guy! I mean, the guy was mutant-big, comic book big! He looked like a wrestler from TV!!! Please, for the love of God, don't hurt me anymore!!!"

Loki stopped and seemed to consider. "He was in the company of a large man, you say? Can you describe this man? I think we can eschew with any more adjectives like 'huge', 'giant', or 'immense', all right? A large man. I get the picture. What else can you remember about him?"

Isaac racked his brain. He had never thought as hard as he did now. He brought every tiny detail he could remember to the forefront of his mind. Speaking rapidly, as if afraid the information might evaporate into the air, he said, "He was much taller than Alex, and Alex is at least six-five or six-six. This guy was almost a full head taller. You couldn't miss him. He was wearing a black coat and blue jeans. He had on a t-shirt that said 'Death before Dishonor', and a pair of combat boots. He had long hair, I mean all the way down his back, tied up in a braid. Oh, and he had a beard. His eyes were blue, too. But it's weird that nobody seemed to really notice the guy. I mean how do you miss a guy like that?" Isaac stopped suddenly, his face comically surprised at the fact that he had managed to remember so much detail. He looked up hopefully into Loki's insane eyes.

Loki stared off into space, his ruined face taking on a dreamy cast. "That's quite a memory you've got there, young Isaac. I'm surprised you could even see him. Of course, being as close to death as you are you're more open to a wide assortment of, shall we say…input" Loki snapped his eyes back to Isaac. "Did you, perchance, hear the man's name mentioned?"

Isaac again plumbed the depths of his memory. He screwed his eyes together with intense concentration. A memory flickered briefly at the edge of his consciousness, and tried to flit away. Steeling himself with the image of his pen stapling his ball to the floor, he grabbed the memory before it could escape him. He opened his eyes and looked up at Loki's distorted countenance.

"I think I heard Alex calling him Henry. This was

after they had gone into Alex's room, so it was hard to hear, but I'm pretty sure he called him Henry."

Loki sat back on his haunches, looking out of the small window in Isaac's dorm room. He sat that way for some time, his forehead creased with lines as he thought. After what seemed an eternity to Isaac, Loki looked back down at him. There was a grotesque look of almost paternal concern stamped on his face. Gently, Loki reached down and grasped the ink pen. With a sympathetic smile, he pulled it out of the floor and the testicle it had held in place. Isaac was amazed that he felt no pain during this. When Loki spoke, his voice was calm and quiet, the voice of a loving father.

"Isaac, you've been quite helpful. Now, if you can further my knowledge by just a little more, sate my thirst for answers, as it were, I'll be on my way, and you can be on yours. Does that plan suit you?"

Isaac nodded vigorously. There was nothing on the earth he wanted more than to be rid of this maniac with his good humor and two-tone eyes.

Loki looked back out the window, his eyes taking a dreamy, far-off cast. He whispered to Isaac, "Where did the two of them go, Alex and Henry? They obviously are not here or we would not be having this little discussion. I need to speak with them… well, it's Alex I need to speak with. The other…this…*Henry*, I think I need not speak to him just yet." His gaze focused back on Isaac. "There will be time aplenty to speak to *Henry*. And I will have much to say, I assure you. So, where did they venture off to, young Isaac? Into which of the four winds did they bend their backs?"

Isaac was at a loss. He had no idea where Alex and his companion had gone. He was unaware that they had left at all. Isaac had been moderately stoned last night, and had spent several hours after seeing Alex and his giant companion going into Alex's room listening to Imogen Heap on his IPod. Alex could have done somersaults down the hallway naked and Isaac would have been oblivious to the fact. However, he sensed that saying that to this nightmarish hobgoblin would result in an extremely painful death. Licking his lips, he made an educated guess and said, "They headed west out of the building. If I had to guess, they were heading for a bar. Probably the Lucky Pony. It's a bar just across from the University. A lot of students go there to drink, 'cause the beer is cheap." He looked closely into Loki's face, trying to gauge how well he had delivered this crucial lie.

Loki maintained the same hale and hearty smile on his face that he had when he had entered the room. Now, however, the edges of that smile seemed to tighten, and in some incredible way, the creature before Isaac looked like he was smiling and frowning simultaneously. In a sane, gentle voice, he delivered Isaac's death sentence.

"There is nothing as fleet of foot and heavy as stone as the mouth that lies." Loki reached out and grasped Isaac's head in his hands. In a prim voice he said, "And your mother would be ashamed of you, lying like that." Then he squeezed his hands together, and Isaac Macintyre's head exploded like an over-ripe melon dropped from a high building. Blood, brain matter, and mucous flew in ropy jets across the room. Loki took a large spray of blood directly in his face, but he merely smiled and licked the blood from around his mouth.

Dropping the nearly headless body of Isaac Macintyre to the floor, Loki stood and turned from the room. He was stopped by the sight of Sigyn standing in the doorway, a look of grief and horror on her face. She looked from the body lying at his feet up into Loki's eyes. She shook her head sadly. Her voice was clear and rang of judgment.

"What have you become? Always, I've known you to be petty at times, cruel at others. But this... this *carnage* is beyond you. You have stood in the halls of the Aesir, but now you are nothing more than a killer of the innocent, a rabid animal. I am with you no longer. This path, you will walk alone. I am finished with you." With that, she turned to leave.

Loki reacted without thought. He reached out with his left hand and grabbed the first thing he encountered. Without looking to see what it was, he took two long strides towards his wife and thrust the object into her back with all the strength he could muster.

Sigyn looked down at her chest with a look of mild surprise. Sticking out of her gown between her breasts was the bloodied end of a bowling trophy. She slowly turned to face her husband. Loki looked down at what he had used to stab her and began to roar laughter. Sigyn folded gracefully to the floor. She caught his gaze with her own, and her eyes were clear and unafraid. Her voice choked with blood, she said, "I shall be sitting in the halls of the Aesir in moments, partaking of the food and drink of the gods. Where will you be, Trickster?

Killing men like cattle? How honorable and great has grown the mighty Loki. Think of the sagas that will be told of you now, Loki."

Her speech concluded, Sigyn closed her eyes and died. As Loki looked on with growing fury, Sigyn's body faded from view, becoming translucent and then disappearing altogether. Soon, there was nothing left to show she had ever been there. Loki stood in the center of the room, looking down at the place that his wife of millennia had so recently occupied. With a shrug, he walked out of the room and turned down the hallway towards the stairwell. In the distance he could hear the rising swell of emergency vehicles.

As he descended the stairwell three steps at a time, he spared one last look upwards towards the place his wife had died. He shook his head and continued down the stairs. He had places to go and people to torture and kill. His voice echoed up and down the stairwell.

"Stupid bitch could've just filed for a divorce. *Women.*"

Chapter Seven

We crossed the vast final plain that spread out below the mountain in silence. Heimdall seemed to fall deeper within his own thoughts the closer we came, and I had run out of questions to keep the conversation going. I could feel a tendril of excitement and anxiety running up and down my spine, coiling tighter and tighter with every step I took forward. No matter how mad this whole affair seemed, it appeared that I was soon going to be standing before my other father, who just happened to be a god. This was a far cry from how I had intended to spend my day.

At the base of the mountain lay a wide stone road that curved up and around the mountain. It was as big as a four-lane highway. The stonework was impeccable, no mortar held the stones together, but a piece of paper would not have fit between the gaps. The stones were smooth and worn. In the multi-colored twilight, they glittered as if frosted with ice. They were not slippery, however, and we were able to walk up the steep incline easily.

I had always been in very good shape, even as a boy. My football coach had always said that if he had ten more just like me, there would not have been a team to oppose us. At the end of grueling practices that left all my teammates hitching breath and trying not to vomit, I was always fresh as a daisy, with hardly a sweat raised. The assistant coach had often grumbled under his breath that he believed me to be on some sort of wonder drug that enabled me to perform so well. My drug tests always came back clean, and my glare was sufficient to shut him up.

However, the walk up this mountain fastness would have been enough to send a platoon of Nightstalkers to the hospital for treatment of exhaustion, like Green Platoon on steroids. Yet Heimdall and I walked it at a pace that was almost a jog, and never grew weary or short-winded. It was as easy as walking across the level ground of the campus between classes.

As we ascended the mountain, the view of the surrounding countryside became more apparent. The rainbow of light filtered everything within view, turning the vast snow-covered whiteness into a warm and inviting landscape. I turned to Heimdall and said, "I bet this place is awesome in the daylight." He looked around and shrugged. "I don't remember", he replied. "I haven't seen it in the daylight for a very long time."

The comment caught me short. "What do you mean you haven't seen it in the daylight? I thought you never slept."

He shrugged again. "I don't. There was a time when the sun shone on the fields of the Aesir, but I don't remember it. When the Norsemen were converted to Christianity, their belief in us waned. When that happened, the sun set. The last time the sun rose here was long ago." He stopped walking and turned to face me. "Belief is what fuels us, like I said. But when man grows out of that belief, we are doomed to remain as we were, never moving forward nor fading completely away. The gods are much like the toys of children. As those children grow, their toys become less and less important to them. And even though they retain fond memories of them, the toys themselves are set aside to molder in some forgotten attic or basement. We are those toys. I can tell you things that happened from the beginning of time with perfect clarity, but I cannot tell you what happened in the months leading up to my meeting with you at your dormitory. We are like the elderly you place in your nursing homes; recalling events from their childhood with perfect ease, but unable to remember the name of their own children when they come to visit." He smiled sadly. "Does this upset you? From the look on your face, I would say that it does."

I was unable to find the words to answer him for a long time. We just stood there staring at each other in the twilight. After a time, he nodded his head up the road and started walking again. I fell in step with him, my mind churning helplessly. After a long while, I was finally able to speak.

"Heimdall, this world you describe… it's terrible. To be a god, to have the kind of power you wield, and yet to be so… I don't know… sad, it just seems so horrible to me. If I were doomed to live out this kind of existence, I would *welcome* Ragnarok, just so I wouldn't have to live this way."

Heimdall turned to look at me, his eyebrow raised. "What makes you think that we *don't* look forward to it?"

I was stunned for a moment. "But you're trying to do everything in your power to stop it from occurring."

He shook his head. "No, we're not. We're just trying to stop it from coming before its appointed time. All things balance out in the end, Alexei. We, the gods, are just the manifestation of that. Believe me, little brother, when the day finally comes that I set myself against Loki, I will welcome it with a gladdened heart. Only then, will I be free of these chains that bind me."

I went silent for a time again as I digested this. The whole thing seemed to be diametrically opposed to itself. Everything was a contradiction. I found myself wishing I had taken more philosophy classes.

Heimdall was watching me from the corner of his eye. He began to laugh. I turned to him, my confusion evident.

"You're having a bit of a hard time dealing with all this, aren't you? I know it's a lot to try to internalize, but you must proceed on faith that all of this makes sense, at least in a universal manner."

I shook my head. "Whatever you say, big guy. I think it's ignorant, but this is your playground."

He laughed again and slapped me on the back. "All things will become clearer to you in time, little brother."

I muttered under my breath. "That's what people have been saying to me all my life."

We continued up the road and were nearing the summit before Heimdall spoke again. "Alexei, when we arrive, you need to be aware of a few things. You are not going to be welcomed in with open arms by everyone here. Some of the gods think that the Norns have gone mad to hinge our fates on a mortal. Some of them are jealous of you, in fact."

I was confused. "Why would a god be jealous of me? That makes no sense."

"They are jealous because you upset the order of things. Were it not for you, they feel that this would have never happened. They feel that the mortal line of Odin should have been eradicated long ago, because it was an anomaly. There are stories aplenty of the gods birthing mortal offspring, but they are just that, stories, myths. In reality, Odin is the only one of the Aesir to have ever done such a thing. There are gods in Asgard that feel that by not only producing a mortal family, but by guarding it all these years, the Allfather has cause the very rift in the universe that allowed Loki to escape his fetters. They do not say this to his face, of course. None of them has that kind of courage." He shook his disgustedly. "At any rate, you need to understand that not all of the Aesir are your friends, even if they appear so. Be on your guard, and remain watchful."

"Which gods should I be looking out for? For that matter, what exactly should I do even if I know who has it in for me? These are *gods*, remember? I'm just a big redneck from a little town in Kentucky."

He held up his hand to stop me. "No, little brother that is *not* all you are. You are the son of the Allfather.

In your world, that meant being larger and stronger than everyone else. Here… no one really knows *what* it means. It may mean nothing at all. You may be, as you say, a simple mortal. This is unexplored ground for all of us. This has never happened before. Like I told you, you are the first mortal to pass Bifrost and enter Asgard whilst still a living man. This uncertainty has made many of the gods more worrisome than usual. With Loki unfettered, there was already much consternation here. When the Allfather sent me to collect you… well, things were made all the more confused. Confusion leads to anger, little brother. I'm afraid this won't be quite the family reunion it should have been." He said this last apologetically.

"So what do I look out for? Whom do I trust?" I asked.

"Well, you can trust me, obviously."

"Really? And why is that?"

He seemed surprised. "Well… do you have any doubt that I could have torn you to pieces in your dorm room, had that been my desire?"

Thinking back to how he had filled the room, I shook my head. "No, I guess not. You could have stomped me like a bug."

He nodded. "Yes, I could have. However, I did not. I answer to the Allfather. His will is mine. There are those among the Aesir that are not so quick to follow his commands, but follow them they do. You can trust the Allfather, as well, but I imagine you don't need to be told that." He looked the question at me.

"No, I don't need to be told. If he's really my father, I guess I can trust him."

"You can. He has wanted to see you for a very long time, but out of respect and love for his wife, he has remained away."

I felt a shiver of fear creep up my neck. "Uh… speaking of his wife…"

"Frigg?"

"Yeah. Uh… she's not exactly gonna be pleased to see me, is she?"

Heimdall smiled. "Frigg has forgiven Odin his transgression long ago. She bears neither you nor your family any ill will. She is the very embodiment of compassion and love. Believe me on this."

"Okay, if you say so. I've just read too many stories about evil step-mothers, I guess."

"She is not your step-mother. She has no claim to you or power over you. You are independent of her in every aspect. Still, she will not shun you, nor attempt to bring you harm."

"Okay, then. So, who am I looking out for?"

Heimdall seemed hesitant to answer. Finally, he blew out a deep breath and said. "Thor is not your friend."

Oh, just great, I thought. Out loud I said, "You telling me that the baddest of all the Norse gods wants to kick my ass?"

He looked up the roadway, his eyes distant and troubled. He nodded slowly. "It's not just that he want to 'kick your ass', as you so eloquently put it, it's that he believes that involving you is an insult to all the Aesir."

Heimdall looked me in the eye. "But it is the affront to his own honor that Thor feels the most. As the strongest of us all, he feels that the job of recapturing Loki should fall upon him, not some mortal son of the Allfather. His pride is hurt. And, as I've told you, he is not very smart. To be that powerful, and not have the intelligence to temper it has always been Thor's bane. Go wary around him. He is easy to anger."

Heimdall must have read the distress on my face, because he clasped me warmly on the shoulder and said, "Fear not, little brother. Thor is strong, this is true, but even *he* bends a knee to the Allfather, and you are here at his behest, and as his honored guest. There will be no open attack against you. Just do not expect help to come willingly from all sides, do you understand?"

I nodded and we walked the last of the roadway. We crested the mountaintop and I was struck mute by the wonder of it. From a distance, the buildings sitting atop this eagle's nest had seemed impressive. Up close, they boggled the mind. It seemed impossible that such things could even exist, they were so massive. Carved from oak, the timbered buildings covered acres of the mountaintop. Seeing my jaw hanging on my breastbone, Heimdall gave a mighty laugh.

"What did you expect, little brother? This is not the home of your Brad Pitt or your Tom Cruise! This is Asgard, home of the Aesir!"

He swept his hand out over the massive fortresses in front of us.

I looked aside at him and couldn't help but pop his bubble a little.

"Well, yeah, they're impressive, but I bet your heating bill is a complete *bitch*."

He did a double-take and then threw back his head and roared laughter. Finally subduing, he motioned me forward. "Come, little brother. Let's go meet the family."

Straightening my spine and squaring my shoulders, I said with a calm confidence I most certainly did not feel, "Lead on, bro."

Together, we walked towards the hall of my father..

Chapter Eight

Loki sat atop the roof of a rest area off Interstate 75, about forty miles outside of Lexington, Kentucky. He hummed off-key as he watched the flow of humanity come and go into the rest stop. It was nearing dusk, and he had been sitting on the roof of the building for over an hour. He hummed to contain his rage, to focus his energy. He had seriously depleted himself earlier that day with the destruction of the dorm at the University of Kentucky. That alone set his teeth on edge. There was a time when he could have brought the whole of the building down by merely thinking it, but no longer.

His years of torment had left their marks on more than just his face. When he had arisen from the smoking ashes of the mine shaft that had so helpfully broken his fetters, he had instantly attempted to open a portal to Asgard. His rage at that moment was so complete that he cared not a whit if he had landed on the dining table of the Allfather himself. Millennia of captivity and torment had done nothing but fill him with madness and rage. In retrospect, he supposed it was something of a gift that he had been unable to open the portal to Asgard, because he would have entered eagerly and been dispatched by the Aesir. Loki had no intention of being recaptured.

When he first realized that he had grown too weak to command the portal to take him to Asgard, he had flown into a rage. When he had managed to calm himself enough, he tried a different tact. He tried to open a portal to Jotunheim, the land of the Giants. He had always had a special bond with the Giants. However, his attempt to enter their realm was met with the same failure as his attempt to gain access to Asgard. For a time it seemed that he was doomed to walk the earth of Midgard with no one but his stupid cow of a wife for company. The very thought of that made him wish for the captivity he had endured for so long. Then he realized that the stupid cow of a wife was no longer a factor, and this cheered him slightly.

Now, sitting atop this squat brick building just off a busy highway, he pondered his options. He could not gain access to Asgard, or Jotunheim. He was sure that any attempt to get into Niflheim or Hel would be met with the same results. None of the Nine Worlds were open to him except Midgard, apparently. Not being able to get into Hel angered him the most, since it was his daughter Hel that ran that kingdom of the dead. It seemed that he was robbed of all of his resources, stuck here on this miserable pile of stone.

He thought long and hard. Dusk turned into night, and a cold rain began to fall. He ignored it. Finally, after many hours of contemplation, he hit upon an idea. Perhaps he could not open a portal, but that did not mean that he could not commune with those that could.

Closing his two-tone eyes, he sent out a message into the black void between the worlds.

Baugi... hear me, Baugi...

For a long moment, there was nothing but the endless whine of wind that forever swept the blackness of the void. Finally, through the wind, came a voice.

Who calls to me?

Loki smiled.

It is I, Baugi. Surely time has not erased your memory of your friend Loki.

Silence once again spun out.

Loki is fettered beneath Midgard. Who is this, and why do you dare impose on me?

True, I have been long fettered. But I am no longer so. I have need of you, Baugi my old friend.

This time the silence held a palpable contempt.

Were it truly Loki that speaks to me now, why would Baugi bother with him? What use is the Trickster to me? I have no need of you, regardless of your need of me.

Loki contained his anger by taking a series of deep breaths. He did, in fact, need this lout, and angering him now would serve no purpose. However, time had not erased the slyness for which he was famous.

Well, it saddens me that one I thought to be my friend would so callously speak. So be it. I had hoped to help Baugi regain some of the honor lost when the deceiving Odin took from Suttung the Mead of Poetry. Or has Suttung forgiven his brother Baugi for his role in this treachery? Did not Baugi help Odin to claim the mead through when Odin tricked him?

Now the silence was filled with menace and rage. When the reply came, it was so forceful that Loki was rocked back on his heels and nearly dislodged from the roof.

NEVER will I be forgiven that!!! Suttung reminds me daily of those evil doings! Speak not of it again, be you Loki or no!

Loki sat back up and wiped his eyes. The mental equivalent of an earthquake had left him with tears of pain in his eyes. He reminded himself to go softly, lest this connection cause him undue pain.

A million apologies, Baugi. I meant not to re-open old wounds. I had hoped only to be as a salve to them. If you are not interested in returning the treachery of the Allfather to him, I will bother you no longer. A thousand pleasant nights to you, Baugi of Jotunheim.

Loki began to break the mental link between them, but he did so slowly. As he expected, he heard the increasingly plaintive cries echoing across the void.

Wait! Wait, I say! How would you help Baugi do this? The cursed Allfather is in Asgard, surrounded by the Aesir. What can Loki do? Any attempt to enter Asgard will only wind up with Loki fettered again in the bowels of the earth, and worse, Baugi with him!

Loki decided to overlook the Giant's thinly veiled insult for the time being.

Do you think so little of Loki, then? Answer me this, then, Baugi: How is it that Loki no longer remains captive? Is it not evident that Loki has grown stronger than even the Aesir? It was they that fettered me, and yet I remain so no longer. It was they that sought to keep me confined until the coming of Ragnarok, and yet I am free. What say you to that, Baugi?

There was a pause as the Giant thought. Like most giants, he was stronger than he was intelligent. Loki waited patiently, buffing his nails against his cloak. Finally, the voice answered.

Loki is free of his fetters. The Aesir are not preparing for war, so Ragnarok is not in the offing. These things tell Baugi that something has occurred, something that the Aesir were not prepared for. Perhaps Loki speaks truly. There was a brief pause, then Baugi continued, his voice laced with contempt. *However, if Loki now speaks truly, it would be for the first time.*

Loki decided that he had taken all the insults from Baugi he intended to. Focusing all his will, he sent his message across the void and into Baugi's mind with twice as much force as Baugi had used on him.

Perhaps that is so, Baugi. Taunt me once more, and you will know just how powerful I have become. Believe that to be truth.

Loki sensed the screams of Baugi as the pain lanced through the Giant's head. Loki hoped that no further lesson needed to be given, because this last had nearly sapped him of all his strength. Blood flowed freely from both of his nostrils, and his head felt as if it were about to explode as poor Isaac Macintyre's had earlier that day.

Please! No more! I beg you, mighty Loki! You are indeed grown strong in your captivity! What need you of humble Baugi? I will do all that I may in service to you.

"About time, you sniveling pile of offal", Loki said aloud, his voice clotted with blood and phlegm. Mentally, he sent *Calm yourself, Baugi. I wish only what you wish. To see the mighty Aesir brought low and humbled before us. Odin has wronged us both with his high-handed and deceiving ways, and he must be brought to task for it. With your assistance, I shall be the tool of that. Will you join with me on this? Shall we two deliver justice to those who think themselves above it?*

The answer was instantaneous and full of wild hope.

Yes, Loki! I am yours to command! What do you need of me?

Loki thought for a moment. What did he need of this slow-witted behemoth? Well, to provide him with passage between the worlds, to start with. Baugi might not be intelligent, but even one as slow as he would find it odd that this newly-powerful Loki could not even summon the ability to flip between worlds. Finally, he sent his answer back.

Baugi, my friend, I need only the simplest of things from you. However, it is not wise that we continue to speak thusly. There might be those that would be listening in, and I have no intention that our plans be made known before their time. Know you a place in Midgard called "Kentucky"?

Loki could sense the confusion in Baugi. *No, wise Loki, I know it not. Is it a mighty hall of your devising?*

Loki blew out an exasperated breath. Leave it to the Giants to take no interest in anything beyond their own front doors.

No, Baugi, it is not a hall. It is a state in a country called the

United States of America. It is beyond the Great Sea of the North, far from the homeland of the Norsemen. One discovered it many years ago, one called Leif Eriksson. Know you this name?

Vaguely, wise Loki. I take little interest in the affairs of Man. They are pitiful, weak creatures, below my wonder.

Well, know you of him now, for I have told you of him. Can Baugi find this land of America, this state known as Kentucky?

I know not, Loki. I rarely venture beyond the borders of Jotunheim.

"Of course you don't, you imbecile", Loki said in disgust. "Every time you do, you wind up making a bigger ass of yourself than the time before." He sent back in thought *Never mind this, Baugi. Can you focus on me?*

Yes, Loki, I can do this.

Then do so. Focus on my thoughts and bring you here to me. Loki stopped for a moment, thinking. It would not go over well for a Giant to suddenly appear at a busy rest area. Humans would see him, and would bring down a thunderous herd of lawmen and reporters. In another time, Loki would have loved nothing better than to be author of such chaos, but not now. A low profile was needed here, and Baugi's sudden appearance would not fit that bill at all.

Hear me, Baugi. I will link with you again when it is time for you to come to me. Do not attempt to link up with me. I shall send for you when I am ready. Be prepared for my call. When you hear it, you will come to me at once. Do you understand this?

Yes, Loki. But why do we meet in Midgard? I have little love for the animal Men. They disgust me.

"And I bet they wouldn't think you looked like Alexander Skarsgård either, you ugly bastard", Loki muttered. He closed his eyes and sent his thoughts back across the void.

Do not question me, Baugi. I have reasons enough for not wanting to have this discussion in Jotunheim. Not everyone can be as trusted as can Baugi.

Loki could sense the Giant swelling with pride and self-importance.

It will be as you say, Loki. I await your command.

Good. Now, leave me to finalize my plans. Be prepared when I call for you. You will not need to come armed for battle. Not yet, at least. Our first moves will be stealthy. A frontal attack is not what I wish. The Aesir will be humbled, but we will not need brute force to do it.

Loki was sure that the Giant wouldn't understand a word of that, as brute force was all he was capable of. Nonetheless, the Giant would obey him, and that was enough.

I await your call, wise Loki.

Good, Baugi. Your reward for your loyalty will be a thousand fold.

Let me but see Odin on his knees, and I will consider my reward paid in full.

That you will see, my friend. You have my oath upon it.

Loki broke the mental connection and sat back, taking deep breaths. It would take all his innate cunning to maintain the façade of strength in front of Baugi. If the Giant even suspected that Loki was not as strong as he said he was, this little ploy would end abruptly. Most likely with Loki's head hanging from a pike in Baugi's mead hall. No, this would take all the finesse and resources available to him. He felt no fear, however. He was the most cunning and sly of all creatures. He would use the foolish Giant to serve his needs, and then dispose of him when the time was right. He lay back on the roof of the rest area, closing his eyes and drifting off to sleep. As he slid into slumber, a single thought followed him.

He needed to free Fenrir the Wolf, from his equally unfair captivity.

He needed to free his son.

Chapter Nine

As I stood before the massive wooden doors to the hall, I couldn't help but shudder. The very size of the place was enough to make a person feel insignificant, but the motif was not something that lent itself to a welcoming aura. The doors were made of giant planks of oak, bound with iron. Intricate knot work had been carved into the sides and top of the door. It was, in a way, beautiful, if you could overlook the fact that human skulls were embedded in the doorframe at intervals. Heimdall noticed my hesitation and said, "This is your father's hall. It is called Valhalla, the Hall of the Slain."

I nodded my head towards the skulls. "Yeah, I can see that. Not the kind of place that you'd be apt to find in *This Old House*, is it?"

"Death means different things to different cultures,

Alexei", he said. "The Norse believed that dying in battle was the greatest of honors. They believed that if they died bravely then the Valkyries would seek them out on the battlefield and bring them here, to Valhalla. It is here that the Einherjar call their home."

"Yeah, it's great, I'm sure. What do they do for kicks on the weekend, kill baby seals?"

Heimdall grinned. "You're not as far from the truth as you think. Each dawn, the Einherjar would meet on the plain and do battle with each other until they are all dead. In the evening, they arise, resurrected and enter the hall to dine and drink mead and tell of heroes and exploits past. It is in this manner that they train for the coming of Ragnarok." He broke off, staring at the darkened plain. "At least that is the way things were, before man lost his faith in the Aesir. Now, there *is* no dawn. The Einherjar sit within, each man drinking mead and staring at the fire in sadness and disgust. Without the belief of man, the cycle cannot be continued." He shook himself, and seemed to rouse himself from his reverie. "Come, little brother, let us not stand out here in the cold. Within is food and drink, and the company of loyal friends."

"Maybe *your* friends. I doubt if I've got very many home boys in there."

He smiled. "Well, if you have no friends within yet, then you shall have some soon. These are the finest of all the Norse warriors. To have them by your side is an honor without parallel. Come, let's go inside."

He pushed the massive door open with one hand,

and it swung silently on well-oiled hinges. He stepped boldly through the door and I had no choice but to follow him, or stand outside in the cold. I took a bracing breath and followed him inside.

If anything, the interior of the building looked even larger than the exterior. I knew that logically that didn't make sense, but since I was standing in the mythical Hall of the Slain about to meet my father the god, I decided to check my logic at the door. The roof was so high above my head I had trouble seeing it in the light thrown off by the thousands of torches burning in wall sconces. The roof looked like it was made of hundreds of thousands of interlocking shields, each with a different design emblazoned on it. The rafters of the building were giant spears, each one longer than a dozen Greyhound buses parked nose to nose. All along the walls were benches, and each of these was covered in various pieces of armor. Breastplates, shields, arm bracers and grieves, along with pile upon pile of chain mail littered the benches. About halfway down the hall was another door. A huge wolf lay in front of it. And by huge, I mean just that. The wolf looked to be four or five times the size of your average tiger. It raised its head when we entered, and seemed to mark me with its eyes. Then it laid its head back down and went to sleep. Over the door, perched on the frame was an eagle. It was just as big as the wolf. It looked like it could carry off an elephant, should the need arise.

Closer to us was a vast open fireplace. Over it hung a cauldron that looked like it would take an Olympic-sized swimming pool to fill it. A gnarled old man tended it, occasionally stirring the contents. From the cauldron came an enticing aroma of meat. My mouth began to water. Lowering my voice, I asked Heimdall, "Who's the old guy cooking dinner?"

He looked over and said, "That is Andhrimnir. He is the cook of Valhalla. It is his job to feed the Einherjar."

"What's he making? It smells great."

"He's making what he always makes. Every day, he cooks the boar Saehrimnir. That is the food of the gods."

"He cooks the *same* boar every day? Is that kind of like the way the Einherjar kill each other every day, but get back up to do it again?"

"Yes. Everything is a cycle, or was, when Man held to his belief in us."

We came around a massive column and I finally got a look at the Einherjar themselves. Heimdall hadn't been kidding. These were some of the meanest looking sons of bitches I had ever laid my eyes on. Each one of them looked like he could eat a platoon of Navy SEALS for lunch, and there were *thousands* of them sitting and eating at the long tables that stretched the length of the hall.

To Heimdall, I whispered, "How many Einherjar are there?"

He nodded towards the doors set recessed along the walls. He said, "There are five hundred and forty doors. Come Ragnarok, there will be eight hundred Einherjar come out of each one, ready to do battle."

I did some quick arithmetic in my head and said,

"Four hundred and thirty-two thousand men? Jesus, who could stand against that many of *these* guys?"

He smiled sadly. "There will be more than just warriors involved during Ragnarok. Trust me; we will need each and every one of them."

I nodded, not knowing what else to say. As we walked down the length of the hall, I noticed that the noise of the warriors had tapered off to muttering. A hush had fallen over the whole assembly. I had never felt more in the spotlight than I did at that moment. If it were possible, I would have dug a hole, jumped into it, and pulled the dirt over on top of me. Four hundred and thirty-two thousand sets of eyes followed us as we walked towards the head of the table. I stood as erect as I could and walked with as much pride as I was able to muster. I hadn't asked for any of this, but be damned if I was going to look like a coward in front of these men.

As we approached the head of the table, I got my first glimpse of Odin. He sat perfectly still, a statue. At his feet were two white wolves, and on each shoulder perched a raven. He was a giant of a man. Even sitting, he seemed to be at least six feet tall. When we reached the end of the tables, he slowly stood.

He was about six inches taller than as I was, which in my current state made him nearly ten feet tall. He had long snow-white hair and a beard to match. He wore a patch over one eye, a leather patch with a rune embossed on it. I didn't know what the rune meant, if it were special to him, or merely decorative. From under his white, busy eyebrow, his single eye pierced me with its strength and fire. It was the color of the sea where it meets the ice. He was dressed as we all were, with chain mail armor, leather tunic, and fur. His helmet rested on one of the peaks of his high-backed chair. There were no horns upon it, no wings. Looking around, I saw that none of the helmets had any sort of adornment like that.

"We would not be so foolish as to give our enemies something to grab on to in the heat of battle", he said, surprising me. "Were I to have horns on my helmet, you might be able to wrench my head around and deliver a killing blow."

Astounded, I gaped at him. I was finally able to stammer out, "Did you just read my mind?"

He smiled. "No. That is not within my power. I merely watched you. You were looking at our helmets. The modern stories and movies made about us have us wearing ridiculous things like horns, wings, things such as that. I have just told you why we would not do such a thing."

I nodded, not knowing what else to say. Thankfully, Heimdall was there to jump into the breach.

"Allfather, allow me to present Alexei Addison. Alexei, this is Odin, the Allfather."

I had no idea what I was expected to do. While I was still struggling with whether to curtsey, bow, or shake his hand, Odin reached out and placed both of his massive hands on my shoulders. He stood there looking me over for several minutes. Finally, his gaze returned to my face and his face creased with another smile. "You have the look of your mother's people."

I smiled tentatively back at him. I was about to speak when what I thought at first was a bear growling made me snap my head to my left. Even as I did, I realized that the growls were actually words.

"His mother's people were just that… *people*. Nothing but half-blood *mortals*."

I looked on in awe as the owner of this new voice unfolded himself from his chair. While nine feet tall seemed to be normal for this place, this individual had to be eleven, if not twelve feet tall. To describe him as massive would be akin to calling the Grand Canyon a ditch. He had flaming red hair and his waist-long beard was shot with gold and copper. He stood with his arms crossed, looking daggers in my direction. It was more than obvious he would like nothing better than to pull me into tiny pieces and toss me in the fire.

Heimdall's warning shot through my head and then left just as quickly. I suddenly found myself furious. I was in a perfect ecstasy of rage. I had been jerked from my normal life and thrust into a situation that even now I was having trouble believing was real. My world had been turned upside down and given a brisk shake in the last twenty four hours, and now this circus strongman was giving me the Evil Eye? Fuck *that*.

I heard Heimdall say warningly, "Alexei…"

I brushed him off with a brusque wave of my hand. I turned to face my opponent. I put my hands on my hips and looked up into his furious face.

"Let me guess. You're Thor. Right?"

"That's right, little human. I am the Thunder God."

I nodded. "Wow, that's really something. A Thunder God. I've never met a Thunder God before. But I'll tell you something. I *have* met my fair share of assholes, and I'm pretty sure that you fit neatly into that category. So, what's your problem, hot shot? You got something against me in particular, or are you just a bastard to everybody?"

The words hadn't even left my lips before some part of my mind politely informed me that it quit, consider this its two week notice. I was stupefied by my audacity, but a more visceral part of me was savagely glad that I had egged on this giant. *C'mon, you big sumbitch, let's see what you got!*, the capering, suicidal part of my mind was howling. I was beginning to think that I had gone completely out of my mind. *You're a super-genius, Alex,* I thought. *You just went and pissed off the meanest of all the Norse gods. Way to go, hero!*

My words had a galvanizing effect on Thor. His hair began to crackle with electricity. To say his muscles bulged was a bit of an understatement. He lifted his hammer, Mjollnir, threateningly. He positively loomed over me. The part of my brain that had recently tendered its resignation put in one final plea for me to run like hell, but I ignored it. If this giant was going to bash my head out of my ass, he was going to do it with me looking him in the eye.

Thor advanced until he was within inches of me. He leaned down until our noses nearly touched. His voice was gravel pouring down a steel chute. "Little human, have you a death wish?"

It took all my composure not to step back. I continued to meet his stare unflinchingly. The part of my mind that was engaged in my continuing well-being had begun to gibber and weep quietly. To my bone-deep surprise, I remained furious. I actually *wanted* to throw down on this guy. *Maybe he's right*, I thought. *Maybe I do have a death wish*. Giving my voice all the sarcasm I could muster, I said, "I don't know, big guy. Why? You think you're the man for the job?"

Thor roared into my upturned face, the expulsion of his breath blowing my hair back. I felt like Bugs Bunny in one of those old cartoons where he tries to take on a bear. Thor raised his right arm and swung it with enough force that I could hear the air parting as it descended. Mjollnir was speeding inexorably towards my face. When it landed, I had no doubt that my skull would simply disintegrate into a hammersmash of blood, brains, and bone.

But still I remained motionless. Call me stupid.

The giant hammer came slicing down in an arc…

And then it stopped.

Or so it seemed to me at first. But as I looked closer, I could see that the hammer was still on its deadly mission to smash in my face, but it had slowed to the point that it seemed to have stopped. I looked around and realized that everyone was in a state of almost suspended animation. I could see Odin opening his mouth to shout, his single eye alight with fury. Heimdall was in the process of reaching for me, to pull me out of the way. I looked down the tables and saw the Einherjar all moving sluggishly to their feet, many reaching for their weapons.

Well, this was an interesting turn of events. I raised my hand and saw that I was still moving at a normal speed. Mjollnir was now less than an inch from my face, and moving slowly closer. I stepped to the side and waited to see what would happen.

The moment I was clear of danger, time resumed its normal course. Thor slammed Mjollnir into the space I had inhabited only seconds before. A look of stupid surprise came over his face, and he jerked forward, off balance with the strength of his heave. He staggered forward and tripped, falling face-first into the stone floor. Odin's voice now rang out, the fury rapidly changing into confusion. Heimdall nearly lost a hand, reaching for me when I was no longer there. Mjollnir came within inches of sheering his hand off.

And then, silence.

Every eye in the hall set upon me, and a look of shocked confusion was shared by thousands of faces. I looked back, unsure of what had just occurred. From the stone floor came the most horrid scream of rage I had ever heard, or hope to ever hear again. Thor bounded up, his face red with embarrassment and fury. He whipped his head from side to side until he found me. With a roar, he hurled himself at me, his hands now empty. It was apparent that he intended to crush the life out of me with his bare hands.

Again, just before he could connect with me, time slowed to an almost stop. I could get used to this. I walked around his airborne body and reached down to pick up Mjollnir. I was amazed at its weight. If that thing had connected with my face, there would have been no way to identify me with dental records. This guy was playing for keeps. As it had before, time resumed normalcy the moment I was out of danger. With a massive crash, Thor found himself on the floor again, skidding several yards.

He bounced back to his feet again and turned to face me. When he saw his hammer in my hands, he went completely nuclear. He reached out his hand, and I felt the hammer wrenched from my grasp. It flew back to him and suddenly appeared in his hands. *Great*, I thought, *a giant sledgehammer boomerang. Can this get any better?*

Thor was breathing hard and staring at me with disbelieving eyes. "Are you a warlock, human? What manner of man can move as you do?"

I shrugged. "I'm not a warlock, Thor. I'm not your enemy, either. What do you say we stop this before someone gets hurt? This is foolish."

The huge man stood very still, his head bowed as he thought. I cut my eyes to the left and saw Odin standing with his arms crossed across his chest. His face showed equal measures of anger at Thor and pride in me. I felt my heart contract. It seemed silly to me that I would long for his approval, but I would be lying if I said I didn't.

Finally, Thor raised his head and looked at me. In a much quieter voice, he said, "I ask you for your pardon. I have acted rashly. My anger toward you is not justified. I am angry, true, but the anger is directed at myself. I should be able to find and fetter Loki myself.

That I cannot has filled me with despair and disgust.
Will you accept my apology?" He reached out his
massive hand towards me. Looking abashed, he added,
"Brother?"

I stepped towards him, mindful that this could be a
ploy to make me drop my guard and attack. However,
this new-found talent of mine for manipulating time
should stand me in good stead if he intended me any
further harm. I grasped his hand in my own and said,
"There is no need for apologies, Thor. I am as much in
the dark about what to do here as you are. I'm sorry if
my presence here causes you grief, but remember that I
didn't ask for this any more than you did."

He nodded. "Well spoken, son of Odin. I have
underestimated you. I am not the most intelligent of the
gods; that I will freely admit. My temper is often the
cause of my own pain. But although I may not be as
quick as some, I am able to admit when I am wrong.
Your ability to elude me shows that there is more to you
than just mortal blood. If the Norns deem it appropriate
that you be here, it is not my place to question them."
He turned to Odin. "Father, I have wronged a guest in
your hall, and a brother to me in blood. What judgment
will you give me for this transgression?"

Odin stared at Thor for several long moments. In a
quiet voice, he replied, "Alexei has forgiven you. In this,
he has shown compassion and fairness. Were I to
punish you now, I would stain that." He paused,
thinking. "This is my judgment, then. You will remain
by your brother's side until he says he needs you no
longer. It will be your task to answer all questions he
may have, and to acclimate him to our ways. Do you

accept this judgment?"

Thor nodded soberly. "I do so, Father. I will be his right arm in all things until this crisis is at an end." He turned to me. "Does this please you?"

I smiled. "Having the mighty Thor as my personal tour guide to Asgard? How could I not be pleased?"

He smiled back, almost shyly. The whole of the hall let out a held breath, and men began talking again. Soon the walls reverberated with the sounds of several thousand conversations. Odin sat at his place at the head of the table, and motioned me to sit beside him. Thor sat opposite me across the table, and Heimdall sat next to me. He leaned over and whispered in my ear, "And just what was *that*, little brother? Have you any other tricks you might enthrall us with?"

I shrugged uncomfortably. Aside to him I said, "I have no idea what the hell just happened. I thought maybe you might know. Has anything like that ever happened before?"

He shook his head. "No. I have never seen such. You appeared to cease to exist in one place, only to reappear in another. You truly have no idea how you did this?"

Helplessly, I shook my head. He stared at me for a moment, and then shrugged his shoulders. "It matters not. At least not right now. It seems a handy tool to have at one's disposal, however. For now, eat and drink." He gave me a conspirator's wink. "I think you'll find that the mead of Asgard packs a bit more punch than the pitiful brew you've been drinking. I would watch how much I drank, unless you want to be rubbing your face on the cobblestones later."

I grinned back at him. "If I get too drunk, you can carry me out of here across your back. I'm not gonna worry about it. It looks like the End Days are here, and I'm gonna try to do my dead-solid best to get completely soused."

I settled down into my chair and nodded my thanks at Andhrimnir as he ladled out a large hunk of meat from a serving platter. I had never eaten boar, but I figured it wouldn't be much different than the pig roasts I had attended. My first bite showed just how stupid that thought was. The flavor seemed to literally explode in my mouth. There aren't words to adequately express how incredible it was. It was as if every good thing in my life had been concentrated into this one piece of meat. Practically drooling, I washed the bite down with a huge gulp of mead from a drinking horn.

If my first taste of Asgardian boar had been intense, then my first drink of the fabled mead left me slack-jawed with wonder. I found myself wanting to jump up on the table and make up an ode to the wonder I felt. However, my eyes crossed and I slumped in my chair. There would be no bounding up on the table for me. My new family and friends all took a look at me and roared laughter. Heimdall helped lift me back into place and gave me another wink. "I told you to go easy, did I not, little brother?"

I wasn't sure which one of him to answer, so I just answered both of him. "You'sh rawt... thish's increbidle...indicrble...incredible!" I looked up at him proudly, grinning like an idiot. "I fink...*think* Imma goin' to taker eashy, okhayy?"

He grinned back at me. "It will pass, little brother. You're the first mortal to drink the mead of the gods in millennia. Try to eat a bit, it will help."

This was easier said than done. My drinking prowess on Earth might have been something to behold, but I was way out of my league here, and I knew it. Fortunately for me, the initial feelings of intoxication swept over and through me, and then settled down into a warm, comfortable glow in my middle. I was able to eat a bit more, and like Heimdall had said, it helped. Soon, I was able to follow the conversation going on around me without having to concentrate all my effort to figure out what was being said.

The bulk of the talk was about Loki, and what was to be done about him. It soon became apparent to me that these individuals had no more of an idea what to do than I did. In an odd way, I found this comforting. The overall sense of otherworldliness and oddity was beginning to finally recede. As difficult as it was to believe, I was actually sitting in Valhalla, drinking with the gods. If my high school guidance counselor could have seen me now, the little prick would be pissing himself.

During a lull in the conversation, Odin looked over at me and said, "Have you any thoughts on this, my son?"

The question took me off guard. I thought about it for a moment, and then said, "It seems to me that until

Loki is… what did you call it? Fettered? Until he's fettered again, everything is on hiatus. Although like I told Heimdall, it seems to me that's not a horrible thing. I mean, if he can't enter Asgard, no Ragnarok. No Ragnarok, nobody has to die. What's so terrible about that?"

A silence fell over the assembled men again, and Odin looked at me with a glint of disappointment in his eye. I looked around for help, but I could see that same disappointment mirrored in the eyes of every person in the room. When Odin spoke again, his voice was soft and almost sad. "Would you so easily shirk your duties, relinquish your honor? Is this what it is to be a man of your time?"

I could feel my face filling with blood, and shame clamped its burning hands around my heart. I lowered my face, trying to escape that look of genial contempt I felt all around me. Finally, I raised my face to Odin and spoke, my voice contrite and apologetic. "Forgive me, sir. That was not the point I was attempting to make. It merely seemed to me that if the Norns didn't foresee this happening, then maybe there is a reason for it. I don't mean to insult your honor or courage, any of you. I would proudly fight and die by your side, if that were called for. I just don't know if that will be necessary. I mean, since the Norns didn't foresee this occurring, then maybe it was meant to be this way. Is that not possible?" I looked around the table again, this time the question clear in my eyes.

Odin answered me, his voice still calm and soft. "No, my son, this is *not* the way it is supposed to be. Each second Loki is loose upon your world, he causes a rift in the very fabric of existence, a rift that grows and grows. Soon, your entire world will be in chaos and ashes. All you know and hold dear will be no more. Ragnarok is for us here to contend with, not the race of man that has moved beyond us. If we do not recapture and re-fetter Loki, all of Midgard will fall. In his hatred of us and his inability to reach us here, he will cause destruction on your world the like of which it has never seen. Do you see now why this must not be allowed to happen?"

I thought about my parents, living peacefully in their little home in Columbia. Then, unable to help myself, I saw that house ablaze, my parents' bodies lying bloodied and torn; a desecration. I could feel rage boiling in my body, rising from my feet and threatening to blow through the top of my head. I looked back to Odin, my eyes fever-bright with anger.

"When do we go after the son of a bitch?"

For the first time since I had arrived at the gates of his hall, Odin threw back his head and roared with laughter. This was answered by the simultaneous roars of approval from the Einherjar. Thor stood, shaking Mjollnir over his head and shouting with joy. Heimdall only sat with his sad little half-smile, his eyes calm and accepting. When the general uproar had diminished, Odin turned to me, wiping away a tear from his single eye, and eye full of mirth and contentment.

"We leave on the morrow, my son. I know not what we will do to rectify this wrong, but we begin on the morrow. And watch your language, young man." He raised his voice for the whole of the hall. "Feast, my

Einherjar! Drink up! If the Norns allow, we shall all be dead by the sun's setting tomorrow! If this be the last night of this eternal twilight, then let us prepare to see once again the face of the sun, before she is eaten by the wolf Skoll!"

The roar went up again. I felt, for the first time since Heimdall had arrived in my life, as if I were with these men, not apart from them. It was very likely that I would be dead before the next sunset, as Odin had proclaimed, but that didn't faze me anymore. The chance to stand with these men filled me with a feeling of honor and contentment that I had never known in my life. Yes, I might die before the next sunset, but then again…

I *had* gotten the best of Thor. How many people can say that?

Chapter Ten

The sun was staining the eastern sky pink when Loki again called out across the chasm of Ginnungagap, the Void. His summons was answered immediately, even eagerly by Baugi.

I hear you, wise Loki. What do you ask of Baugi?

Loki hesitated for a moment. He was standing beside a broken-down barn in the middle of a huge tobacco field. There were no human habitations within view. Still, he was hesitant to bring Baugi into Midgard in his physical form. A giant stood out here, no mistake. Still, if he was going to further his plan, he would need Baugi to open the portal between worlds. Shrugging, he sent out his telepathic command.

Feel you my essence, Baugi?

Again, the answer was immediately forthcoming.

Yes, Loki. I feel you.

Good. Bring you then to me. Come alone, and come without arms. As I said, I have no need of brute strength as of yet.

But, wise Loki, I will be at the mercy of my enemies, should I come unarmed.

"You'll be at my mercy, you mean, you son of a fatted sow", said Loki, grinding his teeth. It seemed that Baugi had been working on his intellect for that last millennium. Wasn't that grand?

What enemies could stand against mighty Baugi here on

Midgard? It seems to me dishonorable that you would even show fear of the pitiful creatures of this world.

The answer was laced with cold venom this time.

It is not the weakling Men I fear, Loki. Why is it so important to you that I arrive unarmed? Perhaps wise Loki has not been as truthful as he says he has been. Fear you Baugi's blades, Loki?

Loki had been afraid of this. Baugi really wasn't stupid, as far as giants went. That wasn't really saying much, but Baugi possessed a keen sense of self preservation. With an inward sigh, Loki responded.

You hurt me, Baugi. You wound me with your unfair words. If it were my desire to see Baugi dead, then dead you would already be. Have we not discussed this when last we spoke? Is there another lesson that need be given?

It was Loki's turn to tinge his words with thinly-veiled threats.

No, Loki, no further lessons need be given. You must try to understand. While I would love nothing more than to trust Loki fully, this request that I come to you without the protection of my arms makes me uneasy. If Loki can give me a good reason for it, Baugi would understand more clearly.

"I don't want you showing up on Midgard ready to kill everything you see, you damned imbecile! Hel take you!" Drawing in a deep breath, Loki calmed himself.

Very well, Baugi. I asked that you arrive unarmed so as to not put the mortals of Midgard on their watch. We must retain a very low profile. I want no one on Asgard to hear of our plans. You know how closely the hated Allfather watches this miserable place. But if you are still unconvinced that Loki wishes only to help Baugi enact his vengeance on Odin, then come you armed to the teeth. When the weak mortals of Midgard see you covered in armor and axe, we'll just explain that you are an actor in a play, how does that sound? I'm sure they would have no problem believing that a Giant such as yourself is merely a jester of the court. Surely Odin won't hear of your grand entrance then, will he?

There was a significant pause as Baugi weighed Loki's words. Finally, his voice echoed across the Void.

Very well, wise Loki. I come to you unarmed. I will trust you in this, that we are brothers in the same cause. But know you this, and heed it well: If your heart is faithless, and you would kill Baugi, I will do everything in my power to bring you with me into the eternal night. Have we and understanding?

Loki shook his head. This is what it had come to? Empty threats from a behemoth on a pride-trip? Loki ground his teeth into a fine powder in his seething rage. Finally able to respond without obvious rancor, he sent his message out.

You need feel no fear of me, Baugi. I want that which you want. Now, focus upon me, and bring you here, so that we may begin our plotting and planning. The time of the Aesir is at an end.

Loki concentrated his energy into a focused beam of thought and sent it winging across the chasm. In a few moments, he observed the air in front of him begin to shimmer. Within seconds, the shimmer had turned into a searing heat from which stepped Baugi, the Giant.

It had been millennia since Loki had last been in the

presence of a Giant, and he almost took an involuntary step backward. He had forgotten just how huge these creatures were. Baugi wasn't even large, by Giant standards, but he was easily twenty five feet tall. He looked down at Loki, a slow smile beginning on his lips, only to curdle when he took in the full measure of the ruin that had once been Loki's face.

"Loki... what have they done to you?"

Loki shrugged it off. "It matters little what they have done to me, it is what I will now do to them that we need concern ourselves."

The Giant nodded, unable to take his eyes from the ruined visage that had once been handsome. Loki gestured for Baugi to sit, to ease their talk. Loki had no intention of craning his neck up to talk to the Giant, and besides, the darkness would not hold for much longer. Loki had no desire for Baugi to be seen on Midgard in the full light of day. Such would reach Odin's ears far more quickly than Loki wanted to risk.

Baugi sat cross-legged and waited patiently for Loki to tell him what the plan was. Loki walked back and forth in front of the Giant, finalizing his plans before he vocalized them. Finally, he turned to Baugi and said, "Know you my son?"

The Giant seemed confused for a moment. "Which son do you speak of, Loki? I know of Narvi, he who was killed by your other son Vali when the gods turned him into a wolf." The Giant's face darkened. "Vile things, the unfair judgments of the gods."

Loki nodded. "Indeed, they are as unjust as they are

cowardly. However, you are not far from the truth. It is neither Narvi nor Vali of which I speak, but I do speak of my other son. He, too, is a wolf."

Baugi's eyebrows shot up in surprise. "You speak of Fenrir? He who is bound by rope Gleipnir on the island Lyngvi in the middle of the lake Amsvartnir?"

Loki gave Baugi a look so cold that the Giant flinched at the sight of it. In a calm voice, he said, "I was unaware I had any other sons so bound. Thank you for reminding me."

Baugi held up his hands uneasily. "I meant no offense, wise Loki. It is only that Fenrir is to remain bound until the coming of Ragnarok. As such, I do not see what he has to do with our plans."

Loki arched an eyebrow at the Giant. "Do you not? Is there, perhaps, anyone else that was supposed to remain fettered until Ragnarok, but is so no longer that you know?" The Giant looked confused. "Someone that escaped his fetters? Someone you are talking to right now, you damned fool???"

Baugi's eyes cleared. "Of course, Loki. You have escaped your torment, so Fenrir can also escape his. Where are we to meet him?"

Loki resisted the powerful urge to send a blinding bolt of energy into the buffoon's ignorant face. Between clenched teeth he spat, "We will *meet* him where he is *bound*, fool! We will free him! And together, we will muster our forces and seek out the help of Surt." Loki's eyes took a dreamy cast. "All of Asgard will burn before us, and the Aesir will scream so loudly that it will cause the very mountains to collapse into the sea."

Baugi had begun to look nervous as soon as Loki mentioned freeing Fenrir. From all he had heard, the Wolf was mad beyond comprehension, and might turn on his rescuers as easily as the Aesir. But when Loki mentioned the fire Giant Surt, defender of Muspelheim, Baugi began to actively fear where this plan was heading. Swallowing the lump that had suddenly formed in his throat, he asked Loki, "Are you sure such actions are wise, Loki? I wish nothing more than to see the Aesir put in their proper place... but to place Surt in our plans? He is mad, or so it is told. He cannot be trusted or contained. And... I mean no disrespect, wise Loki... but your son...Fenrir... he is not... well. I am sorry to put it so bluntly, and I am sorry if I have caused you pain, but there's the truth. You want to bring in to our plans two of the most powerful and uncontrollable creatures under the sky...should we do such a thing?"

Loki stood staring at Baugi in the slowly brightening day. When he spoke, his voice was as deadly as a pit viper. "You call my son mad? You dare insult my son, in my presence? Please, simple Baugi, explain to me what gives you the courage to do this."

Baugi felt the sweat spring up on his face. He stuttered and stammered for a moment, and then regained enough composure to look Loki in his dancing, multi-colored eyes. "Loki, again, I mean no disrespect to you, nor your children. But facts are facts. That you dislike them doesn't change them at all. Fenrir is gone mad. Like you, he was unjustly bound. But unlike you, he has not retained his mind. I have heard it said that even with a sword holding his jaws apart, his roars are unending and shake the very ground. He would run wild the moment we released him from his torment. He might not even recognize us as friends; or you even as his father. We would be hard pressed to control him, once he was free his bindings. I say these things not to draw anger from you, Loki. I say them because they must be said. I get no joy from saying this."

Loki stood contemplating the Giant. He wanted to blast the bastard's head cleanly from his shoulders, but he could not refute the logic behind the Giant's words. After a time, he said calmly, "Very well, Baugi. This deal I will make you. Once we arrive on the island of Lyngvi, I will but remove the sword in Fenrir's jaws. We will speak to him together, you and I. If you are not satisfied that he is worthy of our quest, then we will leave him as he is. I will have the peace of mind knowing that I have at the very least eased my son's suffering, and you will have the peace of mind knowing that we are not enlisting the help of a mad creature." Loki stopped and raised one finger. "However, if Fenrir is capable of thought, and can be useful in this endeavor, you will do two things, Baugi. One: you will apologize both to myself and to my son, and Two: you will never again question my judgment in any way. Are we agreed?"

Baugi thought over Loki's proposal, but couldn't find any logical reason to refuse it. Nodding his massive head, he said, "Yes, Loki. We are agreed. How will we proceed from here?"

Loki stared off into the distance. After several long minutes, he shook his head and looked back to Baugi.

"You will open a portal to Lyngvi. Then we two will see how the land lays. I have heard nothing of a guard there, so we should be able to enter and leave undetected. Does this meet with your approval?" This last was colored with sarcasm, which was lost entirely on Baugi. The Giant nodded his head and raised his awesome bulk off the ground. Dawn had completely broken by now, and Loki was edgy and ready to be off. Baugi began the process to open the portal and then stopped. Turning a confused eye toward Loki, he asked, "Why does not Loki open the portal? Surely such is within his power."

Loki chose to ignore the suspicious look Baugi gave him. He was prepared for this question. Rounding on Baugi, he said in a matter-of-fact voice, "I do not wish to play right into the hands of my enemies, Baugi. Think you that the Allfather would not notice my presence in the Void? If I were to open the portal, he would know instantly where I was, and where I was going. However, Baugi is beneath Odin's interest. Why would the great and mighty Allfather care where goes Baugi? Thor, perhaps, might notice such, but he is slow-witted. By the time he even got around to noticing your movements, we would be there and gone again. Think you that I have not foreseen all this?"

Baugi nodded, accepting Loki's answer without further thought. In front of the Giant, the air resumed its shimmer. Baugi heaved his massive bulk through the portal, and Loki stepped neatly into the space that had been occupied by the Giant. The air wavered and lost its shimmer.

And with that that, Loki was gone from Midgard.

Chapter Eleven

The sound of thousands of snoring men brought me awake. I raised my head slowly from the fur that had had been used as a pillow and took in my surroundings. From my perspective, lying on the floor, it looked like the aftermath of a Bacchanalian orgy combined with the Wehrmacht attack on Poland. Bodies lay all about the place, some on the table, some on the floor, and one for some reason hanging from the large torch-bearing sconces that ran the length of the wall. That unfortunate soul was hanging upside down, his foot caught in the metalwork of the sconce. I didn't envy *his* headache this morning.

Or was it morning? The windows outside showed the same blackness that they had earlier. Confused, I sat up and rubbed sleep from my eyes. Then it hit me. I was in a place of perpetual twilight. There would be no sunrise. I couldn't tell how long I had been sleeping. For that matter, I couldn't recall most of what had transpired the night before. There were hazy recollections of battles, the ring of sword and axe on shield, the frenzied cries of encouragement from the men in the hall. Christ, had I actually been *sword fighting* last night?

As I rose from the bed of furs, I was slapped in the face by the reality that yes, I most certainly had been. There was a veritable Canadian sunrise of bruises covering my whole body. There was blood crusted on the side of my head, and my left hand had swelled to about three times its normal size. I made my way unsteadily towards the table, and sat down with a groan. It felt like I had been eaten by a dragon and left as a pile of droppings on some desolate moor.

A hand placed a drinking horn in front of me and I looked up to see Heimdall grinning smugly at me. I pried one eye open, flakes of blood falling on to the table. I looked down at the horn, and then back up at Heimdall. When I spoke, my voice was foggy and hardly recognizable as my own.

"Do you actually think I'm going to drink this? Are you serious?"

Heimdall plopped down beside me on the bench and swept aside some of the platters from the night before. The sound reverberated through my skull until it felt like a gang of dwarves on crystal meth were building suits of armor between my eyes.

"Heimdall," I pleaded, "Just kill me or something. But please, please, *please* do it quietly, okay?"

He laughed. "I warned you, little brother. Our mead packs a bit of a punch. You acquitted yourself quite well, though. The Einherjar are quite taken with you. I myself was quite impressed with your progress last night. Although I'm not sure that Thorken will be as pleased to see you this morning." He nodded his head toward the man suspended from the wall sconce. My eyes widened in alarm. "You're not gonna tell me that *I* did that, are you?"

He grinned again. "Oh yes, little brother, you most certainly did. Thorken seemed to have the better of you. He beat your sword thrust down with his shield, and then clipped you a nice one alongside your head. We thought we were going to have to step in when you got... agitated, shall we say? You flung your sword and shield to the ground and picked Thorken up and flung him into the wall, head first. His foot got caught in the sconce, and he's been there ever since." Heimdall looked over at the man in question. "You know, I imagine his head is going to hurt far worse than yours does this morning." Heimdall pushed the drinking horn towards me. "Drink, little brother. It will ease your pain."

I gave him an incredulous look. "Look, Heimdall, if I even *try* to drink that, I'm going to spew every bit of that boar from last night all over this table."

Heimdall shook his head. "Another one of the properties of our mead is its ability to heal one's injuries." He paused and smiled. "Both physical *and* emotional injuries. I'll be sure that Thorken gets a big drink before he remembers who hung him upside down for the evening. That should 'grease the wheels', as your kind say."

I gave him a suspicious look, and then sighed. There was no way I could feel any worse, at least. Closing my eyes, I took a tiny sip. The mead tasted as good as it had the night before. My spirits bolstered, I took a more hearty drink. I was gulping it quite rapidly when Heimdall reached over and snatched it from my hands.

"Hey! I was drinking that!" I cried indignantly.

"Yes, you were", he replied affably. "And if you had continued to do so, you would be trying to find your legs in a little while. The Allfather is prepared to head out this morning to find Loki, and I doubt that he would be very pleased if his youngest son was too drunk to sit a horse."

I started to grumble, but then realized that I did, in fact, feel much better. My headache was gone, and the rainbows of bruises were fading from my skin. I felt like I could take on the world. I stood and stretched my back, satisfying crackles running the length of my spine. Looking around, I saw the rest of the Einherjar arousing from their slumber, stumbling towards the table and grabbing their various drinking horns with clutching fingers. I grinned, until I noticed Thorken struggling to right himself from the wall sconce. A little shot of trepidation ran down my freshly-cracked back, but I squared my shoulders and went to help the man down. Heimdall caught me by the arm and swung me around. "The Allfather would like to speak to you", he said. "I'll see to Thorken." With a wink, he headed toward the struggling man. Feeling a bit like a coward, I walked to where Odin and Thor sat at the head of the table, scrolls and parchments laid out all around them.

"Heimdall said you wanted to see me?" I asked as I neared them. They both looked up from their contemplation. Odin nodded for me to sit beside him. I did, and he pushed one of the parchments toward me. I picked it up and studied it, once again amazed that the runes inscribed on it made perfect sense to me. As I read it, I realized that it was written like a military dispatch. It gave place-names and times, along with a brief summary. While I could read it easily, the content eluded me. I looked up at them, my confusion clear in my eyes.

Odin sighed. "It seems that Loki has found a way to cross between the worlds", he said heavily. "We still do not know how he has managed this, but he has left Midgard. We cannot figure where he went, but we know that he is now capable of moving between the worlds again." He gave me a loaded look. "You understand what this means, do you not?"

I nodded slowly. My thoughts of putting Ragnarok on the back burner were pretty much trashed. If Loki could move from world to world, he might come knocking at the gate any minute. Looking around at the host of assembled warriors, I doubted that was going to happen. But it was still disconcerting to know that he had gotten around the very large obstacle of traveling between the worlds. I asked Odin how such a thing could have taken place.

"Do not underestimate Loki. Ever. He is the most cunning and deceitful of all creatures known under the stars. He makes your Lucifer look like a child."

I shifted uncomfortably in my seat. "He's not really *my* Lucifer, you know…"

Odin cut me off with a wave. "Regardless. My point is that Loki is eminently capable of using all manner of things to his advantage. Also…" He trailed off, looking sadly off in to space.

"What is it?" I asked.

It was Thor who answered. "Know you Loki's wife?"

I nodded. "Yeah, her name is Sigyn. She's the one that sat over him while he was fettered and kept the venom from the snake from dripping on his face." I paused, thinking. "You know, that sort of devotion and loyalty is rare in my time, and she's been doing it for over a thousand years."

Thor rumbled his assent. "Yes, Sigyn is a most fair lady, and her loyalty is boundless as the sea. Or was, anyway."

I looked at them, confused. "What do you mean? What's happened?"

Odin looked up at me, his one eye showing his weariness. "After her years of loyalty and love, Loki repaid her by stabbing her in the back with a... what was it called, Thor?"

The giant man growled. "A bowling trophy, Allfather."

I gaped at them. I wasn't sure I had heard right. "What do you mean; she was killed by a bowling trophy? What does that mean? Do you guys even know what that *is*?"

Odin continued to stare at me balefully. "As far as I was able to ascertain, it is a prize of some sort given in a game of skill in which one rolls a heavy ball toward pins. Is this not correct?"

It felt like we had taken a freight train into Weirdville. "Well, yes, that is what bowling is, but how could she be killed by a bowling trophy? I mean, that's insane!"

Odin nodded. "Yes, that is much what we thought. However insane Loki may have been when he was fettered, it seems that he has become far more so with the passage of time." He looked off into space. When he spoke again, he voice was soft with disbelieving wonder. "To so callously kill one that has shown naught but love and dedication for so long... I cannot conceive of it." He snapped back to the present and began looking through the parchments again.

I couldn't help myself. "But what happened to Sigyn? I mean, she's a goddess, right? You can't just kill a goddess with a fucking bowling trophy, it's too absurd to even imagine!"

Thor glanced up at me. "No, brother, you cannot kill a goddess with a 'fucking bowling trophy'" He gave me a glance that made it clear that my language was still in need of some fine-tuning. "But you can destroy her will to live. The betrayal she has had to endure will not leave her long in Asgard. Already, she is dissipating into nothingness." He sighed heavily. "I fear there is little we can do for her. Would that it were not so, for she is a lovely woman." His eyes hardened. "One more reason, if one was needed, to recapture this creature and increase his torment all the more."

"Where is she?" I asked. "I'd like to see her, if I may."

They both looked at me oddly. Finally, Odin asked me gently, "Why, my son? What good do you think you can do?"

I thought for a moment. Finally, I shrugged and said, "I don't know. I just want to see her. I want to see... I don't know. It just seems like a thing I have to do. May I see her?"

Odin and Thor exchanged a look. Odin nodded slightly, and Thor came around the table and took me by the arm. "Come, brother", he said. "We will go to where she lays. If you think there is something you may do to change her decision to allow herself to fade, then it must be tried."

We walked towards the door, but were met just before the entrance by Thorken, he looked daggers at me. The mead had not had the hoped-for effect. He squared his shoulders and lay a hand on his axe. His voice was as cold as the dead man he had been for a thousand years. "You and I have matters to discuss. Now."

I looked him in the eyes and said in a flat voice, "Later, you and I can finish our discussion. Right now, something more important has come up. I will see to you as soon as I can. Now, stand aside."

Thorken showed no intention of moving aside. His voice hot with fury, he said, "There are no matters more important than the honor of Thorken. I have been an Einherjar for over a thousand years. The Valkyrie picked me up from a battle field in which I sent over twenty to meet the gods. I will not stand aside for the likes of you. Now, draw your weapon, or I will cut you down where you stand."

I didn't think, I just acted. I don't even remember

thinking about what I was going to do before it was done. My right hand shot out and grabbed Thorken by the throat. Although he outweighed me by at least fifty pounds, I lifted him into the air with one arm as if he weighed no more than a feather pillow. Thorken savagely twisted and tried to free his axe from his belt. I could feel my rage building again, as it had the night before, starting from my feet and welling up my body. I dimly heard a collective gasp and suddenly realized that I was no longer holding Thorken. He remained pinned to the wall in front of me, his feet several feet off the floor, but I was not touching him physically in any way. Instead, pulses of blue light were emanating from my hand and slamming into him in a rapid succession. Instinctively, I knew that if I wished, I could burn him from the inside out, leaving nothing but a pile of ashes. I could barely recognize my voice when I spoke.

"And now, Thorken, son of Beornor? Will you stand aside for the likes of me now, or do you want me to fry you like a chicken? Answer me, damn you!"

Thorken was trying to answer, but he couldn't get any words out of his throat. The blue bands of light were searing into his flesh, deeper and deeper with each pulse. I felt a strong hand on my arm, and a voice crying out to me desperately. Shaking my head like a wet dog, I cleared some of the rage from it. I turned to see Thor, his eyes huge, telling me that that was enough; I had made my point, release the man!

I turned back to Thorken, who was now barely conscious, smoke rising from the ring around his throat. In horror, I dropped my hand to my side. I felt sick. Thorken fell to the floor with a thud, and didn't move. I looked around helplessly. The Einherjar were all giving me a wide berth. Only Thor remained by my side, his voice soothing me, calming me. My eyes misted with tears. What in the hell had I done?

I stepped towards the splayed body of Thorken, who was trying to breathe, a thin tea-kettle whistle coming in and out of his throat. Many of the Einherjar made a low grumble and hands went towards weapons. I didn't think to tell them I meant no more harm. A few stepped forward, their fearlessness a tribute to their character, given what I had just done to one of their number. Thor stood between me and them, his eyes flashing. Whatever was about to happen was between Thorken and I, his voiceless challenge said.

Again, I acted on instinct. Thorken's eyes were open, and he stared at me defiantly, welcoming death for a second time. I was amazed by the strength of these men. Kneeling by his side, I said, "Thorken, what I have done is far beyond what was deserved. Allow me to fix it, please." The man looked at me confusedly, not knowing what to make of my calm, reassuring voice. I could see in his eyes that he expected me to finish him, now that he was at my mercy. I took advantage of his momentary confusion to lay my hand across his throat. His eyes bulged with fury, which melted into confusion, and then wonder.

The same blue light that had impaled him to the wall now flowed over his throat. The smell of singed flesh disappeared, and the welts faded from his throat. In seconds, he was hale and healthy as he had been on the day he had died. *Wow*, I thought, *I just saved a dead guy. Whoopee!*

The Einherjar now stood in shock, looking to one another in amazement. Thor kept better control of his emotions, jerking his head towards Thorken. Several of his companions lifted him from the floor and took him over to the table to sit down. Thorken's eyes never left me, his hand rubbing his throat. Thor took my arm again and we stepped through the massive portal and out into the colorful twilight. We walked for several moments in silence before Thor finally spoke.

"What are you?"

I was taken aback by the question. I shook my head. "I'm exactly what I said I was, Thor. Don't ask me how I can do those things, because before yesterday, I've never even been able to do a decent card-trick. I just don't know."

Thor continued to look straight ahead, and he set a killer pace. Even with my newly-elongated legs, I was forced to hurry to keep up. Finally, the silence got on my nerves.

"Well?" I asked, a bitter note in my voice. "What is it? Do you think I'm lying to you?"

Thor simply shook his head. "No, brother, I do not think you are lying. I just don't know what to make of you. We each have powers. You have seen this. It's only that no one has seen powers such as yours. Perhaps it is the mingling of mortal and our blood, I know not. I know only this: You make the Einherjar nervous. By all the gods, you make *me* nervous, and I fear nothing. If these are powers that you didn't even know you possessed, what manner of powers may you still discover?" For the first time, he turned to look at me. There was something in his eyes. Not fear, but wariness. It hurt my heart to see that in his eyes, but I had no idea what to do to dispel it. To change the subject, I asked him where we were going.

He seemed relieved for the change. He nodded his head toward another massive hall in the distance. "Sigyn is there, in Fensalir, the Hall of Frigg. Frigg has taken the watch over her, to ease her pain as best she may."

I felt that little trickle of nervousness. "You know, Heimdall said that Frigg had forgiven Odin for sleeping with my great, great, great, great… oh, hell, my *uber-*great grandmother. But I can't help but think that she might not be very happy to see me. You know what I mean?"

Thor smiled gently. You obviously don't know Frigg. Well, of course you wouldn't, would you?" He laughed. "A gentler and more caring woman never you've met. She holds naught against you for our father's indiscretions. She realized from the moment your ancestor was born that the fault lay not with the child, but with the father. And at that… she cannot remain angry at the Allfather. She is a great woman. You will see. Fear not, brother."

"Is Frigg your mother?"

Thor laughed. "No, my mother is the Earth. She is called Fjorgyn."

I stopped walking. "Okay, let me get this straight. Odin had sex with the earth? How is that possible…

wait, never mind, I don't want to know."

Thor laughed again. "You are still hung up on viewing the world through the eyes of a mortal, brother. Things here do not work the same as on Midgard."

"Well, you'll have to forgive me, big guy. Mortal eyes are the only kind I've ever had... at least until recently."

He nodded. "Things take time to adjust in one's mind. Take me, for example. Yesterday, I had every intention of killing you for a pretender and a conniver. Now, I would lay my life down to save yours. Things change. Fate degrees what it will, and we are fools to challenge it."

"You know, Thor... you said yesterday that you weren't very smart. Seems to me like you're plenty smart enough. Don't sell yourself short, bro."

He gave me a warm smile. "It's not my intelligence that is so much at fault as my temper. But I work at it, and in time I hope to master it."

We fell into a companionable silence for the remainder of the walk to Fensalir. The architecture of the halls was as breathtaking as ever, but I would have truly enjoyed seeing them in the full light of the sun. It would have been a wonder to behold.

We arrived at the door to the hall and Thor very respectfully knocked and then stepped back and waited. After a few moments, the portal swung open and standing in the doorway was a radiant, beautiful woman. Her eyes were soft and compassionate, and she radiated warmth and caring from her very being. Thor nodded his head and said, "Frigg, may I present to you Alexei Addison. Alexei, this is Frigg, wife of Odin." He raised his hand to usher me in. I stood nervously in front of Frigg, my eyes downcast. Despite all reports to the contrary, a very large part of me was sure that she was going to slap me and tell me to get the hell out of her hall, at the very least.

She reached up and placed a warm hand under my chin and tilted it up, forcing me to look her in the eyes. I swallowed audibly, awaiting the firestorm I knew was coming. Instead of knocking my teeth out, she smiled at me. "Alexei. How good it is to meet you. You are a fine, strong young man. Odin's blood is strong within you, I can tell. Welcome to my hall. Please, come you in."

We stepped into the Hall, which was brightly lit by torches every ten feet, and by a massive fireplace at the end of the hall. Frigg motioned us towards some seats and bid us to sit with her. She looked from Thor and back to me. Her eyes were curious, but she waited patiently for us to give our reason for being there. She offered us mead, which Thor took with alacrity. I accepted my horn out of good manners, but sipped very little. I had no desire to repeat last night's drunken stupor. To my surprise, the mead was much mellower, not nearly as strong as that which was served in Valhalla. Frigg saw my surprise and smiled.

"I hope you don't find my mead to be too weak", she said, her voice lilting and melodic. "I don't feel the need to have my feet unable to find their way to my bed at night."

I smiled back. "No, this is really great. It tastes

wonderful, and to be honest, I'm kind of glad it doesn't put you under the table the first drink you take of it."

Thor snuffled with amusement, but buried his laughter in his drinking horn. I cut my eyes towards him and gave him a cool look, but he appeared to be looking at a tapestry on one of the walls. It seemed apparent to me that he was going to let me do the talking, once the formalities had been observed. I took another fortifying drink and looked Frigg in the eye.

"I suppose you're wondering why we're here", I said.

She nodded slightly, her head turned slightly to one side. She crossed her hands in her lap and sat patiently. I took another sip and plunged ahead.

"Well, first off, please allow me to apologize for coming to your home this way. I can't imagine that you have a great deal of love for me or my family, and I hope you don't see me coming here as an insult to you." I looked at her hopefully, praying that I hadn't touched a nerve.

She eased my suffering by laughing, a sound like fine crystal chimes playing gently in the wind. When she had regained her composure, she looked at me with mirth still evident in her eyes. "Dear boy, is that why you seem so ill at ease? Please, trust in me when I say this: I have nothing against you, nor have I ever had anything against your family. They are now, and always have been, fine and honorable people."

'Told you", Thor muttered into his drinking horn.

I gave him a hot look, and then turned back to Frigg.

"Well, yes, he's right. Everyone has told me that you bear me no ill will. It's just that, well… we have a saying in my world. 'Seeing is believing'. I guess I just wanted to make sure I wasn't upsetting to you."

She gave another small, beautiful laugh and said, "Well, now you've seen, and I hope you believe. Worry not, Alexei. We shall be friends evermore, shall we not?"

I smiled at her. "I would like that very much, Frigg. Thank you for putting my mind at ease."

"No, Alexei, thank you for having the compassion and decency to think of my feelings, and to attempt to assuage any anger I might have felt. You're a fine young man, and it is my honor to know you."

We beamed at each other like old friends until Thor cleared his throat meaningfully. With a start, I realized that there was still much to do this day, and we needed to be on our way soon. To Frigg, I said, "I understand that Sigyn is here with you, is she not?" I could feel myself falling into their speech patterns unselfconsciously, and didn't mind it one bit.

Frigg nodded. "Yes, bless the child; she is here in my care. But for how much longer, the Norns only know. She is fading fast. What that… *thing*", she pursed her lips as if she had eaten something sour. "What that thing has done to her is beyond all bearing of that which is right and just. Would that I could lay hands upon him, if only for a moment." Her eyes became as icy as the path that had led me here, and I was completely grateful that I hadn't earned this woman's ire. She looked like an incredibly dangerous cat, one that could strike out and leave a man dripping blood with no warning at all.

I nodded my head in agreement. "Hopefully, before this day ends, we will have our hands on him. If the Norns allow, he will be in our custody soon, and he will pay for all the wrongs of which he is guilty. I give you my oath upon that."

She nodded silently, and I could tell that she was pleased with my choice of words. When she spoke again, her eyes had resumed their original state of calm compassion. "But what is it that you hope to find with poor Sigyn? I assure you she knows nothing of…his… whereabouts. She would be more than willing to tell us all she knew, but she unfortunately knows nothing. *Loki*", she spat, "told her nothing about his schemes. She knew only that he was looking for you, and that he missed you at your dorm. The carnage there was enough to convince her that the man she loved was gone. She turned her back on him to leave him forever. That was when he most cruelly and deviously stabbed her in the back."

My heart jumped into my throat. I took a hitched breath, let it out, and then took another one. My voice quavered a bit as I asked, "What happened at my dorm?"

Frigg shot a glance at Thor, who tried to make himself smaller in his chair, something that was an utter impossibility for someone his size. Frigg's voice held a faint note of accusation in it when she said, "You haven't *told* him what has happened???"

I snapped my head over and gave Thor with a

curious look. "What happened, Thor? What happened at my dorm after Heimdall and I left?"

He looked vainly around for some means of escape, but he was caught, and he knew it. Finally, he huffed, "Well, we saw no reason to upset him further, Frigg. He was already at the end of his tether, with everything that had happened to him. Why upset him further when there was nothing that could be done about it?" He looked defensively at her, and then back at me. "Alexei, there really *wasn't* anything you could do. It happened long after you left with Heimdall."

I could feel my anger rising. "Wasn't anything I could do about *what*, Thor? What happened in my dorm, dammit?"

Frigg made a small sound of hurt as she tried to calm me down. "Please, Alexei, please be at peace..." She got no further. I hated to be rude to her, but I held my hand up to silence her nonetheless. My gaze remained locked on Thor.

"I asked you a question, *brother*. What happened at my dorm?"

Thor's face grew red as his own anger rose to meet mine. With a deep breath, he calmed himself. When he spoke, his voice was mild. "After you and Heimdall crossed Bifrost, Loki arrived at your dorm, with Sigyn. She was unaware of his motives. He found your room. Once he realized that you had already departed with Heimdall, he became enraged. He destroyed your room, and much of the floor with it." Thor paused, looking grimly into his drinking horn. When he resumed, his voice was softer, but full of cold steel. "Loki killed a number of the...ah...warriors? No, *policemen*, policemen that guard your campus, in addition to seven men that were not in class that morning. One of them, a lad named Isaac Macintyre, was tortured by Loki before he killed the boy. Sigyn came upon Loki just after he had committed this murder, and it was then she forsook him and turned to leave. He grabbed the trophy from the boy's desk and drove it into her back. She died a mortal death there, arriving here in a state of what I can only call shocked depression. She has been growing steadily worse ever since." The worst of it over, he raised his eyes to meet mine. "There was nothing that could be done to stop Loki from killing those people. Had you been there, you would have been among their number."

I felt like I had been punched in the guts. I couldn't get a breath. Isaac Macintyre, dead. *Tortured* to death. I could see him in my mind's eye, a portly nineteen year old boy. Dead now, because of me. I finally managed to catch my breath enough to speak. "And you let me drink and have a grand ole time last night, knowing that people had died because of me? What the fuck kind of game are you playing at, Thor? Did Heimdall know? Did *Odin?*"

Thor was obviously not used to being called to task for anything, but he bore it well. "Of course Odin knew. It has ever been his practice to oversee the events of Man. His ravens, Huginn and Muninn, see all and report back to him daily. And yes, Heimdall knew. He is the Watchman of the Gods. It is his *job* to see and know everything that affects the Aesir. But ask yourself this, Alexei: Had you known, what would you have done?

And you are wrong, you know. Those people died not because of you. They died because of *Loki*, the very creature that you intend to help us find, catch, and punish."

I felt betrayed. But even through the hot tears that scalded my face, I knew Thor was right. Had I been there, the only thing I would have done was allowed Loki that which he wanted above all other things: The ability to enter Asgard and destroy everything he could touch. Still, the weight of those deaths hung around my neck like a stone. Isaac Macintyre... Jesus, the kid was just thrilled to be out of the reach of his overbearing mother. Now, he was cooling on some morgue slab somewhere, waiting for his mother to come and collect his corpse.

I struck the tears from my eyes savagely and turned to face Thor. My voice was like broken glass, and each word tore at my throat. "Fine. You may be right. Maybe I would have done nothing more than die there and give Loki what he wanted. But hear me on this, Thor: No more. From now on, *I'll* be the one to decide what I hear and what I don't. Not you, not Heimdall, and not the Allfather himself. Got it?"

Thor stood with quiet dignity. "I serve the Allfather. If you intend to give him orders, they must come from your mouth, not mine. He, like the rest of us, was merely trying to look out for your best interests. If you find fault with that, then you have my apologies for any pain I may have caused you. However, I will do as the Allfather commands me. If you have a problem with that, you must take the matter before him." Having delivered his speech, he sat back down.

"Oh, I fully intend to take this matter before him, believe me." My eyes felt like balls of molten lead rolling around in their sockets. Frigg rose and seemed to glide to my chair. Taking my head in both of her gentle hands, she raised my face to hers and planted a cool and wonderful kiss on my brow. I felt like I had as a child when my mother had given me such magical kisses to make the pain go away whenever I hurt myself. I thanked her silently with my eyes, and she nodded her understanding.

Going back to her seat, she spoke in her quiet voice. "Alexei, I am truly sorry for the pain you feel. But please understand that it was not of your doing. If you feel responsible for this, and you shouldn't, then make it right for yourself by returning that animal to his cage so that he may never harm an innocent again." She paused. Looking me deeply in my eyes, she asked, "But I believe you had a reason for coming to my hall, did you not?"

I took a cleansing breath. Yes, I had a reason for coming here. And time was rushing away from us all with fleet feet. Pushing my pain and inner turmoil aside for the moment, I looked at Frigg and said, "If it is possible, may I see Sigyn?"

Frigg seemed taken aback by the question, but nodded. "Yes, you may see her. I cannot see what it is you hope to achieve by this, but yes, you may see her." She stood and led the way towards the back of her hall. I got up to follow, and after a moment's hesitation, so did Thor. We walked to the rear of the hall, where several doors led off into other rooms. Without hesitation, Frigg knocked gently on the door to our immediate right and then entered. I followed right behind her. Thor hesitated yet again at the threshold, but, shrugging his massive shoulders, he came into the room as well.

The room was filled with the largest bed I had ever seen. It looked like the deck of a ship, with its billowing sails of cloth. Lying in the middle of it, looking ashen and pale, lay Sigyn. Her eyes fluttered as we entered, and she opened them at the sound of Frigg's voice. She turned her head towards Frigg, and I was astounded by the fact that I could almost see through her. It was as if she really was fading away. Her breath was barely perceptible. She seemed to bear no wound, and there was no blood, but nonetheless, she was almost gone. In a tight whisper, I asked Frigg what was happening to her.

Her voice soft and sad, Frigg said, "When Man began to lose his faith in us, we remained. So long as our names remain, if even in myth, we remain as well. But when one of our kind loses hope, loses faith in *themselves*, what you see before you transpires. She is quite simply *believing* herself out of existence." Frigg sighed. "There is nothing that we can do about it, I'm afraid. When such a course is set upon, there is never a turning back from it." A single tear wound its way down Frigg's pained face.

I turned to where Sigyn lay on her yards and yards of fabric. Setting down on the bed, I made my way close enough to her so she could hear me plainly without straining. Almost in a whisper, I spoke directly into the cup of her ear.

"Sigyn, do you know who I am?" I asked.

Her eyes fluttered again, and she looked up at me. She smiled wanly and nodded. Her voice had an odd, muffled quality, as if she were speaking to me from the other side of a wall instead right next to me. "You're the man Loki sought. I'm so glad he found you not. You are safe here. You are among friends."

I reached out and took her frail hand in my own. "You are among those same friends, Sigyn. I would know you, if you gave me the opportunity, Will you do that for me?"

She turned her head and cocked it quizzically. "I don't understand. What do you mean?"

I smiled my most stunning smile at her. "I mean that I would like to get to know you. Is that all right? Will you let me get to know you?"

She smiled weakly. "What would you like to know, son of Odin?"

I caught my breath. This was going to be the tough part. "Sigyn, I want to know *everything* about you. All that there is to know. There is only one small problem, however."

She looked at me, her eyes silently asking the question.

"I cannot take the time to know all that there is to know about you right now, Sigyn. I simply cannot. There is something that I must do that will take me from this place for a time. But when I return, I want you to answer all my questions. Have we a deal?"

She closed her eyes, and a tear slipped out of one and rolled down her cheek. Her voice was barely above a whisper. "I fear that is something I cannot do, son of Odin. My time is nearly done. I cannot return from where I am now. I haven't the strength. I am truly sorry. I feel I am in debt to you. It was my husband that sought your death. He seeks it still. I cannot carry that burden. I am truly sorry, son of Odin."

I was prepared for this. Acting on the instinct that has so far not lead me astray, I whispered in her ear, "Sigyn, you allow yourself to slip out existence because of your lack of faith in yourself. Now, hear me: This I will not allow. You say you feel you bear a debt to me, then I tell you that you can repay it. When I return here, you will tell me of all your life's stories. You cannot begrudge me this simple request."

She smiled at me. "I would not begrudge you anything, son of Odin. But it is too late. I am too weak and far-gone down my path. Would that it were not so, but the Norns have named this my day to end."

I gripped her hand tightly and said, "Well, I'm *un-*naming it! If Sigyn has not enough faith to hold to this place, then I will have enough for both of us!"

My hands began to glow with that same soft, blue light. This time, as with the healing of Thorken, the light pulsed out of my hands and into hers. With each pulse, Sigyn seemed to be more solid, more there. Her eyes snapped open in shock, and she looked at me with wonder. In just a few moments, she lay before me, as vibrant and healthy as she ever had. I heard the gasps of Thor and Frigg, but stared only into Sigyn's eyes. When

140

I had her whole attention, I asked her in my softest voice, "Now, will you remain so until I return, so that you may grant me my request?"

She looked at me with something akin to love. "Yes, son of Odin, I will remain as you have made me. I will accept this gift, and when you return, I shall answer any and all questions you have for me. Does this suit you?"

I smiled down at her. "It suits me fine, Sigyn. Oh, and one other thing: My name is Alexei, or Alex. Let's just leave the 'son of Odin' bit out, all right?"

She smiled at me and I was momentarily dazzled by her beauty. I shook my head to clear it, and climbed from the bed. As I walked past Frigg and Thor, both of whom were still standing in open-mouthed shock, I said over my shoulder, "Remember our deal, Sigyn. I want to see you looking just as you do now upon my return."

She sat up in the bed and looked at me dead in the eye. "I shall remember our deal well… Alex."

I couldn't keep from grinning as I headed out of the room and down the main hall.

Chapter Twelve

Standing on the bank of the island Lyngvi, the dark waters of the lake Amsvartnir lapping the shoreline, Loki and Baugi looked in silent awe at the sight before them. Bound to a huge bolder stood Fenrir, a tiny ribbon wrapped around his massive frame and holding him immovable against the rock. Loki walked slowly towards his son, who was at the moment sleeping. Baugi had no such need to come within reach of the creature, and wisely stood at the lake's edge. Loki had closed within yards of Fenrir when the Wolf's eyes snapped open. Unable to turn his head, his fire-red eye blazed in the darkness as it tried to lock on to the person walking towards him. An inhuman howl echoed across the water, turning Baugi's bowels to jelly. The Giant was more and more wishing he had ignored Loki's call.

Not hesitating at all, Loki walked in front of his son. The Wolf's eyes blazed with madness, and foam dripped from his muzzle. For an uncertain moment, Loki feared that Baugi might have the right of it, that his son was beyond the realm of understanding. Steeling his resolve, he walked straight up to within inches of that horrible maw. The sword that had been lodged in the Wolf's mouth remained in place, having gouged out bloody chunks of meat in the roof of its mouth. Loki felt the warm blanket of rage fall over him at the sight of his son thus treated. He silently renewed his vow to see all of Asgard in flames. Looking directly into Fenrir's eyes, Loki said, "Know you not your father, my son?"

Fenrir looked confused for a moment, and his horrid howling tapered off into a pitiful whine. The Wolf attempted to speak, but the sword lodged in his mouth made such impossible. Loki smiled at his son. "Allow me to remove this terrible thing from you, my beautiful son. Without hesitation, Loki reached into the fetid jaws of the huge Wolf and grasped the sword with both hands. But even with all his considerable strength, he was only able to move the weapon slightly. The movement caused Fenrir great pain, and the Wolf wept tears of fire that splattered the ground at Loki's feet. Unmindful of the flames that nipped at his boots, Loki called out to Baugi to come aid him. The Giant slowly walked over to where father and son stood staring each other in the eye.

"What need you of me, Loki?"

Without taking his gaze from his son, Loki said, "This weapon has an enchantment upon it, a very strong one. I require your brute strength in addition to my magic to remove it. When I give you the word, you will grasp it and pull it from my son's mouth, while I work to remove the enchantment."

Baugi stood, unsure. Loki, still maintaining eye contact with Fenrir, said flatly, "Do it now or die where you stand, Baugi. I am in a mood."

Left with little choice, Baugi reached into Fenrir's mouth and took hold of the sword. While Loki concentrated all his mental effort, he spat, "Now!" at Baugi. The Giant heaved with all his might. There was a sickening rending sound of tearing meat, and the sword flew out of Fenrir's mouth and onto the ground.

With a huge expulsion of rank breath, bloody chunks of flesh flew from Fenrir's mouth. As with all immortal creatures, once the blade was removed, the flesh began to knit itself back together. Within seconds, Fenrir's mouth was healed completely. Shaking his head from side to side, the Wolf looked closely at Loki. His voice somewhere between the roar of a lion and the voice of a man, Fenrir said, "Father? Is this truly you I see before me, or have my wits taken leave of me again?"

Baugi gave a slight shudder at that word "again".

Loki reached up and ran his long, slender fingers through the thick fur of his son's face. His voice barely above a whisper, he said, "Yes, my son, I stand before you. Your father has come for you."

Fenrir threw back his head and gave forth a howl so loud that Baugi fell to the ground, covering his ears and screaming in pain. Loki seemed not to notice. Fenrir, his triumphant rage spent, looked closely into his father's face.

"What have they done to you, Father? How have

they scarred you thus?"

Loki smiled. "Worry not for my scars, my son. The Aesir will pay for each mark in blood, I assure you. How feel you?"

Fenrir trembled against his bindings. "How do I feel? I feel as if I've been bound to this thrice-damned rock for eternity! I cannot remember when last I tasted of meat, or ran across the moonlit sky! Forever it seems I've been here Father! Forever and more!"

Loki continued to stroke his son's face. In a soft, crooning voice, he said, "This I know, my son. I, too, have been fettered thus for a millennia. But now, as you see, I am free. And so soon shall you be, as well."

Fenrir looked closely at his father. "Ragnarok has finally come? The time for our ultimate triumph is finally here?"

Loki shook his head. "No, my son. The Norns are in quite a huff, from what I understand. They have not decreed that Ragnarok has come, and yet here I stand, unfettered and free to take my vengeance."

"But how, Father? If Ragnarok is not upon us, how came you to be free?"

Stepping closely to Fenrir's ear, Loki whispered, "T'was the folly of Man that freed me. I am not as strong as yon oaf thinks me to be. I am using his ignorance and strength to our mutual gain. He believes me to have grown so powerful that I broke free my bindings myself and reentered Midgard. Do not let on that things are not so, for we need the fool yet."

Fenrir gave a ghastly smile, his huge fangs glinting in the half-light. When he spoke, his voice was a low growl. "I hear you, Father. But once we have finished with him here, may I eat him? I have been so long without food, and I, too, need my strength."

Loki looked thoughtfully at Baugi. The Giant was still kneeled over, holding his ears and moaning. Turning back to Fenrir, he said, "Are you able to travel between the worlds, my son?"

Fenrir looked surprised. "Yes, Father. The hated Aesir never thought it necessary to remove that power from me, once I was bound here. How they laughed, Father. All but Tyr. He laughed not." The Wolf's eyes gleamed with insane joy. "I made him place his right hand in my mouth as my term for letting them bind me. This chain…" He looked down at the silk-like ribbon holding him fast with hatred. "This chain was so much smaller than all the others they had used to bind me, and I thought that there was mischief afoot. So before I let them bind me, I demanded that one of them place their hand in my mouth, as a show of good faith. Tyr was the only one of the cowards that possessed enough courage to do so. When I realized that I could not free myself, I snapped his hand off at the wrist and swallowed it down." The Wolf paused, staring off into the distance. "That was the last thing I have eaten in over a thousand years. But at least my last meal was of the Aesir!"

Loki smiled. He began to look at the chain that held his son fast to the rock. It was light as a feather. He gave it a tug, but it held taut. Looking up into Fenrir's eyes, Loki asked, "What manner of binding is it? How can so thin a chain hold my mighty son?"

Fenrir growled into the darkness, his eyes glowing like coals. "It is a chain of deceit and treachery, that is what it is, Father! Thrice they came at me with their chains. First they brought the chain Laeding. It was strong, but I was stronger! I snapped it in their faces! They left and returned with a chain much more massive. They called the chain Dromi. This chain, too, I snapped apart like so many twigs. You should have seen their faces, Father! Such fear on the visages of the *mighty* Aesir." Fenrir's words dripped sarcasm. "But the third chain..." He trailed off.

"What of the third chain, my son?" Loki prompted.

"The third chain the Aesir had forged by the dwarves of Svartalfheim. It is the chain you see before you. When the Aesir asked me if I could break this chain, I told them that there was no glory to be found in ripping apart so fragile a thing. Gleipnir, they called it." Fenrir hung his head in shame. "They used my pride against me, Father. They told me of how the chain was stronger than it looked, stronger than either of the chains before it, but they were sure I would break it, as well. My pride thus engaged, I entered into the pact that one would allow me to hold their hand in my mouth whilst the others bound me." Fenrir looked at his father, pain and humiliation evident in his eyes. "But break Gleipnir I could not, no matter how hard I tried. When I realized I was bound, my only vengeance was to eat Tyr's hand. Tyr had always been good to me, Father. He fed me joints of meat when none of the other Aesir would come near. I am loathe to admit that I feel badly that it was his hand I ate."

Loki grabbed Fenrir's face by the massive mane of fur. He pressed his face to his son's, and his voice hissed out into the darkness. "Never again allow me to hear that you feel anything but hatred for the Aesir. *Any* of the Aesir! They are all a pack of lying, bumbling fools that deserve no less than the pain I will bring them." He stopped, and a slow smile broke across his face. "No, not the pain *I* will bring them... the pain *we* will bring them, my son. Together, you and I will recruit more like-minded allies, and we will storm Asgard and render it unto ash!"

Fenrir, properly chastised, said, "Yes, Father, you are correct. Tyr may have been kind in the past, but he did nothing to stop the torment I faced. We will end their reign, you and I. But first... how will you release me from this binding? I cannot break the chain, and I am stronger than ever I was. How will you break it?"

Loki considered the chain. It was so thin and seemingly fragile; he knew that great magic had gone into its making. He asked Fenrir, "How did the dwarves create it, do you know?"

Fenrir nodded his shaggy head. "Yes, once I was bound, they made great sport of me, laughing and teasing. They said the dwarves had created it using six things: The sound of a moving cat, the beard of a woman, the roots of a mountain, the sinew of a bear, the breath of a fish, and the spittle of a bird."

Loki's brow furrowed in thought. "These things make no sense. Cats make no noise, women bear no beards. How can one find the roots of a mountain? Fish have no breath, nor do any birds in Asgard have spittle.

Only the sinew of a bear is a thing that is real."

Fenrir nodded. "Yes, Father. This mystery I have long pondered while bound here. Of all the things that have gone into its creation, only the sinew of a bear is something that one can actually find."

Loki thought for a long time. Finally, the most cunning of creatures smiled slyly. "The mystery is not so mysterious after all, my son."

Fenrir looked confused. "What mean you, father?"

Loki reached out and touched Gleipnir. "Except for the sinew, all the things that made this binding are things of the mind, my son. The dwarves are cunning in their own fashion. The Aesir were convinced that you could not break free of it because it was fashioned by things that cannot be seen. Your belief is all that holds it in place.

Fenrir looked thoughtful. After a time, he said, "Then what holds me, Father?"

Loki smiled. "The only thing that binds you to that stone is bear sinew, and your own false belief that things that cannot be seen cannot be overcome. Can you break free a chain made from the sinew of a bear?"

Fenrir snorted. "Of course I can! I have eaten more bear in my time than a few! I can pick my teeth with their bones. Bear sinew! That is nothing to me!"

Loki stepped back. Motioning with his hand, he said, "Then break the chain, my son. It is nothing but sinew. Cast off your false belief that it is more, and it will snap like twine."

Fenrir lowered his head and thought for a time. Finally, he raised his head and asked, "Nothing but sinew?"

Loki nodded. "Sinew and nothing more. Trust in me, my son."

Fenrir began to shake and tremble. A growl began in the back of his throat, building in intensity until it shook the ground beneath them. Baugi went back into his crouch, moaning and covering his head. Raising his head to the sky, Fenrir howled, "Nothing but sinew! Now, gods of Asgard, you will feel the wrath of Fenrir!"

With a massive jerk, Fenrir tightened his huge muscles. Gleipnir, the tiny ribbon that had bound him for so long didn't just break, it disintegrated into dust. Free of his bindings, Fenrir jumped into the air, so high that Loki could no longer see him. Suddenly, the Wolf landed on the far side of the island with a massive thud. Wheeling around, he bounded back to his father, covering him with great, slobbering kisses. Loki laughed and embraced his son. They danced and cavorted around the island for quite some time, so full of mad joy at their mutual freedom. Baugi could only watch with mounting concern, his fear that Fenrir was the one that was mad slowly changing to incorporate Loki in that madness.

After the wild abandon had gone on for over an hour, Baugi stood and carefully made his way to where father and son danced. Clearing his throat nervously, he said in a timid voice, "Wise Loki, it is glad that I am that your son is free. Mighty Fenrir, you will exact your vengeance on the Aesir, of that I am certain. But perhaps we should leave this place now. We have been here over-long, and I fear that our presence may be detected by our enemies. Let us be off, to find the rest of our allies in this venture. What say you to that?"

Loki, sweat dripping off his face from his wild dancing, grinned at Baugi. "Loyal Baugi! How wise you are to notice that we have overstayed our welcome on this accursed island! You are quite correct, of course. We must be off. There are many things left to do, and many individuals we must speak with. However, my son has been bound for a very long time. He is a growing boy, as you can see. He must feed before we begin our trek. He'll need to regain his strength, so he will be in top form when we assault Asgard."

Baugi nodded confusedly, not quite sure what the Wolf's dietary needs had to do with them leaving this place. Already, they had stayed too long, and it wouldn't be much longer before the Aesir began to notice something was happening on the island. His voice still trembling slightly, he said, "Of course, Loki. We will find some food for mighty Fenrir, as soon as we depart this place. We can go to my home in Jotunheim and your son can have his pick of my herds. Does this suit you?"

Fenrir began stalking around Baugi. His growling voice became a purr as his said, "Baugi, you are indeed a friend to my father and I. We are in your debt. However", he continued, his voice becoming rougher, "I am afraid that I need to feed now. It has been too long since last I tasted flesh, and I am so very *hungry*."

Understanding far too late, Baugi threw up his massive hands in defense. "Loki", he cried, "Why? I have given you nothing but loyalty, and this is to be my payment?"

Loki smiled warmly at the doomed Giant. "Your service will long be remembered, loyal Baugi. I will have the bards set your deeds to song, never fear." Looking over at his son, Loki said, "Be quick, my son. The Giant is correct. The Aesir may not know we are here yet, but that time is fast approaching." With that, Loki turned and looked out over the darkened waters of Amsvartnir. From behind him, he heard Fenrir's voice.

"I've never eaten Giant before. I wonder how you will taste?"

The sounds of his son feasting caused Loki to smile. Family reunions were always such a touching time.

Chapter Thirteen

Thor and I were about halfway back to Valhalla when we saw Odin and Heimdall at the head of a vast army of Einherjar, all horsed and coming to meet us. We quickened our pace and met them in the middle of the road. Odin looked grave, Heimdall looked thoroughly pissed.

"What's going on?" I asked

Odin blew out a heated breath. "It seems that Loki is far more impudent and daring that I would have given him credit for."

I could feel Thor tensing at my side. "What has he done?" the big man asked.

It was Heimdall that answered. His anger was visible. "The motherless fool has freed Fenrir!"

Thor was taken aback. "How? That's not possible!"

"It obviously *is* possible, because it's happened!" snapped Heimdall.

Thor growled and opened his mouth to retort when Odin raised his hand imperiously. Everyone grew silent, although Heimdall and Thor continued to shoot sparks at each other with their eyes. When Odin spoke, his voice was calm.

"I do not yet understand how Loki has managed this feat. We are going now to the Lyngvi to see for ourselves what has occurred. Will you join us, Alexei?"

I nodded. "Of course I will, Allfather. If we are to find this bastard, we need to find his trail, do we not?" I noticed that Odin had winced slightly when I called Loki a bastard. The sight confused me. After Thor and I had gotten on to our horses and started off toward Amsvartnir, I made my way to Odin's side and asked him about it.

He looked at me for a moment and then sighed. "Long ago, I swore to be blood-brother to Loki. It pains me that we are now so set against one another"

Even though I had heard this before, I repeated it. "Blood-brother to Loki? Why? I mean, if it's none of my business, I understand, but... *why?*"

Odin looked down the road we were on. "Long ago, Loki was not the twisted creature you know him to be now. He was once an honorable creature, and one that I was proud to call my brother." He sighed sadly and shook his head. "We are what the Norns have made us."

I didn't have an answer to that, so we rode along silently for a long time. We crossed the darkened fields of Gladsheim, moving towards Lyngvi. The trip took us just under an hour at a full gallop. Like the men that

rode them, the horses of the Aesir were of a much
larger and tougher breed than anything I had ever seen
at home, and I grew up in Bluegrass horse country. At
the end of a gallop that would have left the fastest horse
on Midgard dead of exhaustion, the steeds of the
Einherjar simply snorted and tossed their heads in
anticipation of more riding.

The place of Fenrir's binding wasn't going to make it
into any tourism brochures, I was pretty sure of that.
The lake Amsvartnir looked about as hospitable as a
week-end at Chernobyl, and the island in the middle
was a far cry from the Bahamas. I was about to ask how
we were going to get to the island when Odin answered
my question before I could ask it by simply riding his
horse into the lake. More accurately, he rode his horse
over the lake, its hooves never actually touching the
water. *Okay*, I thought, *floating horses. And we thought we
lived in thoroughbred country back home.*

We made our way to Lyngvi and sat appraising the
scene before us. The giant boulder to which Fenrir had
been bound was cracked in half and leaning crookedly
to one side. Near the base of it lay the remains of
something that was vaguely humanoid in shape, but
immense. I rode a little closer to see what it was, and
was glad I hadn't eaten anything this morning. Vomiting
in front of the Einherjar would have probably been a bit
of a *faux pas*. Odin, Thor, and Heimdall all rode over to
inspect the remains, as well. There wasn't much to
inspect, truth be told. Most of whatever the hell it was
had been gnawed on, leaving only cracked bones and
blood strewn about. The thing's head was still
reasonably intact, and Thor leaned over his mount to
look closely at it. With an amused grunt, he straightened

in his saddle and said "Baugi", in a smug voice.

I looked over at him and said, "Is that some sort of Old Norse word that means 'Man, that is one jacked-up looking piece of dead thing'"?

Thor laughed and said, "No, that is the 'jacked-up looking piece of a dead thing's' name. What you see lying before you is all that remains of the Giant Baugi."

Odin grinned, his single eye crinkling up in amusement. He glanced over at Thor and Heimdall and said, "I suppose he won't have to listen to Suttung's ravings over the Mead anymore, will he?" The three of them laughed as I looked on in confusion. Seeing my face, Thor told me the story of how Odin had used Baugi to get the Mead of Poetry from his brother Suttung. I shook my head. "I'm really going to have to get used to your sense of humor. And I thought Jim Carrey was funny." I shook my head.

Thor's eyes lit up. "I, too, enjoy the antics of Jim Carrey. He is a truly gifted mortal, and would have made a fine jester at any court. Seen you the film 'Bruce Almighty'?"

I just sat there with my mouth hanging open, wondering if the weirdness of this was ever going to end. When I finally found my voice, I said, "Thor, my brother, I would love nothing better than to sit down with you and talk about the merits of the many works of Jim Carrey, but at the moment, I'm looking at a disemboweled giant and trying to locate a massively pissed-off wolf and a lunatic that want to destroy all of creation. So, maybe another time, okay?"

Odin's smile disappeared. His voice was heavy when he spoke. "Alexei is correct. We waste time here. It is obvious that somehow Loki has managed to free his son. This has upped the stakes considerably. We must move with haste." He turned and motioned for another of the Aesir to come forward. Although Thor was by far the biggest of the bunch, the newcomer was somehow far more menacing. I felt no fear of him, but a very healthy dose of respect. Odin held his hand out and introduced him. "Alexei, this is Tyr. You were... indisposed by the time he arrived last night. You... may not remember meeting him very clearly." The little grin was back, I noticed.

I held my hand out to Tyr and said, "Hi, Tyr. Just call me Alex. I didn't...uh... do anything stupid around you last night, did I?"

Tyr grinned and took my hand. "Well, you would have to clarify 'stupid', I should think. I came in just as you decided that Thorken would look better inverted from a wall sconce."

Great, I thought, *another lasting impression made.*

He looked at Odin, who gave him a slight nod. Tyr trotted his horse over to the boulder and spent several moments pacing the ground around it, looking intently at the ground and sometimes sniffing the air. I glanced at Heimdall and said in a low voice, "I thought Tyr was the god of war. Is he also like the bloodhound of the Aesir?"

Heimdall looked grim as he answered. "No, little brother, he is no bloodhound. It was he and he alone that possessed the courage to place his hand in the mouth of Fenrir when we bound him. For that courage, he lost his hand." Heimdall nodded towards Tyr, and I could make out the fact that his left hand was gone, his arm ending in a leather cap inscribed with runes. Tyr continued to pace around the boulder and surrounding area, and I couldn't help but see the similarity between him and a dog tracking something. When I mentioned this to Heimdall again, he gave me a distracted look. Then the confusion faded and he said, "When Fenrir ate Tyr's hand, he took into himself part of Tyr. Not just the physical part, but a bit of his essence. Tyr has forever since been able to sense Fenrir, just as Fenrir senses Tyr. In this way, Tyr will be able to track the Wolf, perhaps lead us to him."

I settled back to digest this newest bit of oddness until Tyr came riding back. He flicked his chin in the direction of the far shore of Lyngvi and said, "The Wolf ran about the island for a while, with his father. It appears they were dancing. He then devoured Baugi here and then opened a portal near the far shore. The essence of the portal is faint, but it reeks of Jotunheim."

Odin sat silently contemplating this for several long moments. Finally, he looked around at the assembled men and then back at Tyr. "Could you re-open the portal, just enough to give us a view of where in Jotunheim they may be? I do not fancy arriving in the middle of a meeting of the Giants until we are better prepared and with more Einherjar."

That gave me pause. We had better than three hundred of them with us now. If the presence of three hundred Einherjar, Thor, Heimdall, Tyr, and Odin himself was considered an insufficient force to meet the Giants, I was a bit worried about what kind of foes they were. Thor saw my discomfort and laid a reassuring hand on my shoulder. "Fear not, little brother. I have fought the Giants all my long life. They are a stupid lot." He paused for a moment before continuing. "However, they are strong, immensely so. I would not hesitate a second to face any of them in combat, but if Loki has called them together… well, it would be safer to have more warriors with us to attempt such a fight."

I smiled crookedly at him. "You say so, bro. This is your ballgame. I'm just a spectator." Thor looked at me closely for a moment and then said softly, "No, Alexei, I think you are far more than that."

I didn't have a come-back for that one.

Chapter Fourteen

Loki wasted no time with is newly-freed son. Fenrir opened a portal to Jotunheim and they arrived at Utgard, the Citadel of the Giants. Walking boldly up to the massive gate, Loki cried out, his voice booming across Jotunheim, "Open! Open for Loki and Fenrir, for we have business with your king!" From within the fortress came the sound of many Giants moving quickly to the walls. A guard came to the gate and looked down at Loki with a haughty glare. "Be on your way, little one, and perhaps I won't kill you and use your skull as my mead-cup", he growled.

Loki stood quietly and looked up at the guard without emotion. Turning to his son, he simply said, "Fenrir?"

With a savage howl, the mighty Wolf hurled himself over the gate, landing well behind the guard. Within seconds, the hapless guard was devoured, with all the Giants looking on in terror. After several seconds of loaded silence had passed, Loki called out again, his voice now sweetly reasonable. "Open the gate, if you don't mind. I am in a bit of a rush, you see."

The Giants closest to the gate fell over themselves to get the massive portal open quickly enough to suit their guest, spurred on by the menacing growls of Fenrir. With the gate open, Loki calmly walked into the Citadel of the Giants and looked serenely around at its terrified inhabitants. Cocking one eyebrow, Loki asked, "Your king, then? I would be taken to Utgard-Loki without more delay."

Loki and Fenrir were taken immediately before the King of the Giants, the crafty Utgard-Loki. The King was not happy to be entertaining such guests, but after a glance at the foam running off Fenrir's massive fangs, he wisely hid his annoyance. In a calm voice, he said, "So, it is true. Loki has broken free his fetters, and now I see he has unfettered his son, as well. You stand before me, yet Eggther plays not upon his harp, so Ragnarok is not upon us." Loki looked to the King's left to see a grim Giant sitting morosely upon a mound, a harp hanging loosely from one hand. He gave the Giant a nod of his head, and then returned his attention to Utgard-Loki.

"You are well-informed as always, mighty Utgard-Loki. Indeed, Eggther, your watchman, plays not his harp, so Ragnarok has not come. And yet, as you have yourself pointed out, here stand Loki and his son, unfettered and free to seek their vengeance. What have you to say of this?"

The Giant king was silent for several long minutes. When he finally replied, his voice was slightly hushed. "I know not *what* to make of these things, Loki. You and

Fenrir stand here, as you say, and yet the Norns have decreed that such things would not come to pass until the Doom of the Gods." His voice took on a plaintive tone. "How *is* it you have been freed?"

Loki looked at the king smugly. "I am stronger now than ever I was, and so is my son. We live outside the decree of the Norns. Their pitiful forecasts mean nothing to us. We are here, now, to enlist the might of the Giants of Jotunheim to make an end of the callous, arrogant Aesir."

Utgard-Loki was utterly speechless. He stared at Loki as one would a madman. The silence spun out until it became oppressive and hung like a blanket over the hall. Only Loki and Fenrir appeared to be unfazed by it. Loki merely stood looking calmly at the king, and Fenrir let his red gaze travel over the host of Giants as if sizing up each one's caloric value.

Finally, Utgard-Loki spoke, his voice soft with wonder. "It may be possible. If I did not see you standing here before me I would never have dreamed that the long-awaited fall of the hated Aesir could come before Ragnarok… but stand here you do." He fell silent, thinking. Loki let him think. After a time, he looked into Loki's multi-colored eyes and said, "What need you from Jotunheim?"

With an evil grin, Loki rubbed his hands together and began to speak.

Chapter Fifteen

We fell back to Valhalla to regroup and figure out our next move. Odin was grim and silent, and his mood fell over the rest of us like a pall. By the time we arrived at the massive hall, I had begun to feel a sense of helplessness that I couldn't shake. I shot furtive glances at the other Einherjar and I could tell that they were feeling the same. We trudged into the hall and sat around the tables in silence.

After a quarter hour of this, the Allfather seemed to rouse himself and looked around at the assembled men. He stood, and every man in the hall came to silent attention.

"My Einherjar, my sons, and my comrades... we are not furthering our quest by sitting here. I have given this much thought. An out-right assault on Jotunheim is a perilous thing, even more so now that we know that Loki and Fenrir reside in that realm." He broke off and looked about the hall, his eyes taking measure of every man. "However, are we going to let so trivial a thing as the possibility of our destruction stop us from doing our duty?"

A roar went up from the men, and I found myself screaming as loudly as I could. Men slapped each other on the back, and hands were clasped. Weapons left scabbards and were raised into the air and slammed rhythmically against shields. Odin smiled and held up his hands for silence. Once he had it, he looked about once more. With a grin, he said, "In the absence of a solid plan, we will go forth with what we have at our disposal... no plan at ALL!!! Eat, my Einherjar, and see to your weapons! We attack Jotunheim an hour hence!!!"

The hall became a beehive of activity. Men wolfed down food and drink while burnishing their weapons, checking armor, and tightening the leather fittings of their shields and chain mail. Odin had retired to the back of the hall with the other Asgardians and was looking over maps and checking routes. He motioned for me to join them. I came over and looked down at the maps arrayed on the table and asked, "So, we really don't have a plan, huh? Just gonna wing it?"

Thor smiled at me, his teeth gleaming out of the copper of his beard. With a chuckle, he said, "These are the attacks I am best at, my brother. Plans tend to get too... *complicated*. Easier to charge in and kill everything we see."

There was a general laugh at this. Odin nodded and turned to me. "My son, there *is* no plan for a full assault on Jotunheim. There are too many choke points, too many ambushes waiting to be sprung. Our only hope lies in the speed of our attack, and the fact that the Giants are as unprepared for our assault as we are ourselves. If the Norns decree it, we shall be inside the citadel of Utgard before our enemies have an opportunity to mount a serious counter-attack."

I looked at the map of Jotunheim for a moment. I could see what the Allfather meant. Jotunheim was crossed with mountains from one end to the other. Every pass could bottle up an army. Looking at Odin, I asked, "Can't we open a portal to Jotunheim at the gates of Utgard? By-pass all these mountains and arrive at the gates themselves? That should cancel out any ambushes along the way."

Odin shook his head. "A good thought, my son, but one that the Giants have had as well. They know that we would arrive at their doorsteps if we wished to attack them directly. That is why the flat plain that Utgard sits upon", He pointed to the flat land with the citadel in the center of it on the map, "has many enchantments placed upon it. I could open a portal there, but even I could hold it open only for moments. We could not place any more than a handful of our men on the plain before the portal closed again. Those few that managed the plain would find themselves overwhelmed and slaughtered." He sighed. "No, my son, we must open the portal here", again, he indicated the map, "beyond the plain. The enchantments are such that the farther from Utgard the portal is opened, the longer it can remain so. In order to open a portal that would allow us to field an army capable of taking the citadel, we must arrive in Jotunheim here." The area of the map he indicated was easily thirty or forty miles from the stronghold, plenty enough time for the Giants to mass their forces and bottle the army up at any number of strategic points. Looking at the map, I could see all too well in my mind the casualties that would mount at each pass. I swallowed audibly.

Odin placed a reassuring hand on my shoulder. "Fear not, my son. Dying is something that holds no fear for the Einherjar. After all, they've already done it once, have they not?" He laughed at my strained nod. "All will be well, Alexei. Fear not."

He turned and fell into conversation with the Asgardians. They spoke in terms of how many hundred would fall at each pass. A shudder shot through me. I turned to look at the men in the hall, preparing for battle. What would happen to them when they fell in battle in Jotunheim? As Odin had pointed out, they had already died to the mortal world. They would face that death never again. But when they fell in this attack, what then? Would they return here? I asked Odin this.

He stood for a long moment, his arms crossed and his head furrowed in thought. Finally he looked at me, his blue eyes troubled. "I know not, my son. This has never happened before. I have no way of knowing what the fate of these men shall be. They were destined to fight at Ragnarok. The unfettering of Loki has changed everything. All the things we took to be true could now be false. These men died each day in battle, but they awakened at the fall of night to feast again. Or so it was before mankind lost faith in us. It could be that they will, as you suggest, simply return here upon falling on the field. Then again…" He trailed off, his silence saying more than his words. Finally, he shook his head. "They are Einherjar, Alexei. To fight and die with honor is held by them above all things. Whatever fate befalls them this day, they will meet it with the same courage that they have met everything else in their existence."

I was still troubled by the thought of these men falling before the blades of the Giants and then simply... fading into nothingness. At first, the thought filled me with sorrow, but that was soon replaced by a deep, rolling fury. Men such as these deserved better than an iffy future simply because some Norwegian deep miners screwed up and freed an immortal schizoid. I could feel the rage washing over me like the tide coming in. I became aware of the hush that had fallen over the hall in increments. Glancing around me, I was surprised to find every eye in hall on me.

And every eye was about as big as a silver dollar, too.

There was an inrush of air as the men in the hall all gasped at once. I looked down at myself and added my gasp to the majority. As it had done before, blue light was pulsing my arms. Of course, it was pulsing down my legs, too. Ditto my chest, groin... you get the idea. I was awash in that blue light. It brightened and dimmed in pulses that I realized were in time with the beating of my heart.

Odin stood, his single eye staring at me in bemusement. "Something you wish to share with us, my son?"

Suddenly grinning, I said, "Yeah, I think there is. How would you like to field every Einherjar here outside the gates of Utgard?"

He looked confused. "We have discussed this, son. I cannot hold the portal open long enough..." He trailed off and an answering grin rose to his lips. Heimdall gave out a joyous shout. He clapped Tyr on the back and was practically dancing. Thor still looked confused.

Scratching his beard, he said, "What is it? Why is everyone so pleased?"

Heimdall answered him. "What happened when you tried to take our brother's head off with Mjollnir, Thor?"

I watched the gears grind in the huge man's head. Slowly, he said, "When I attacked him, he… disappeared, and then reappeared elsewhere. How is to help us?"

I smiled at Thor. "I didn't disappear, Thor. It was like time had slowed down for everyone but me. You all seemed to be moving in super slow motion, yet I could move at regular speed. Do you see?"

The Thunder God continued scratching his beard. Finally, he let out an exasperated sigh. "No, not really. I don't see at all. I mean, I understand that *you* would be able to move at regular speed, but how would that help us place the Einherjar on the field of Utgard? They would still be moving slowly, you know."

I felt my grin fade. I looked around and saw the same thing happening on the faces around me. With a defeated sigh, I said, "You know, Thor, I wish you *were* as stupid as you think you are. I never thought about that."

Silence fell over the hall again, and gloom moved right back in and unpacked its bags. A few minutes later, however, Heimdall started grinning again. There was something sinister in the way he was doing it, and I asked nervously, "What? Why are you looking at me like that?"

Still grinning wickedly, Heimdall said, "I hope you've got a good, strong back on you, little brother."

And then he started laughing.

Chapter Sixteen

"You want me to do *what?!?*" I asked incredulously.

"You heard me, little brother", Heimdall replied. He looked positively smug, and I wasn't sure if I wanted to laugh at him or slug him in the face. He continued looking at me blandly. "Can you think of a better plan?"

I looked helplessly around for support. Of all the assembled men, only Odin was doing a good job of not laughing, and even he had a tiny smile on his face. I held up my hands, warding off what was obviously a serious case of group insanity. "C'mon, Heimdall, do you have any idea how long that would *take?* Or how exhausted I would be, even if I could pull it off?" Finding no sympathy coming from Heimdall, I turned to Odin. "Allfather… please… talk some sense into your son, please?"

Odin stood stoically, nothing but that tiny grin in his eyes giving him away. When he spoke, his voice was perfectly reasonable. "Heimdall has a point, Alexei. Have *you* a better idea?"

"Well... no, I guess not, but really... I mean, come on, you guys! This is crazy!" I looked imploringly from face to face, and found nothing but mirth. "Oh, *fuck*..."

Twenty minutes later, we were ready. The Einherjar stood in ranks as far as I could see in both directions. I could feel my stomach tightening. The laughter had almost subsided, but occasionally a chuckle would slip out from the group. I sent a scathing look into the crowd whenever I heard one. Smiling broadly Thorken blew me a kiss and said, "Don't be getting too familiar with me now, my lad. We've not reached that point in our relationship." If looks could kill, Thorken would have dropped to the ground and rotted where he stood. The men roared laughter.

Shaking my head, I stalked up to Odin and said, "Well, let's get this show on the road." Half to myself, I muttered, "I... cannot...fucking... *believe* this..."

Odin smiled at me. "What you do this day will be sung about by the bards for a thousand years, my son. The trials of Hercules will pale by comparison. And watch your language. I grow tired of reminding you."

I stared at him, my mouth agape. Shaking my head, I said, "Right. The bards. I can't wait. And you'll forgive me if my language is a bit coarse, given what I'm about to do."

Odin laughed and then grew serious. "Remember, Alexei, once you have finished, you must fall back behind us. You will be in no shape to fight." I gave him a short nod. Around me, the men became serious. It was time to get down to business. I consoled myself by imagining the looks on the faces of the Giants. It wasn't much, but it helped. A little, anyway.

Odin spread his hands and the air began to shimmer in front of him. The portal between the realms opened. I focused all my energy on the portal. Hell, I didn't know if it would even work. If it didn't, this was going to be the shortest invasion in the history of the Nine Worlds.

I felt the energy begin building in me as it had before. And, as it had done before, time fell away to a stop. I was standing in a vast field of frozen statues. The portal remained open, shimmering before me.

I will spare you the details. I'm not even sure if I could explain it if I tried. Needless to say, I spent what felt like an eternity picking up four hundred and thirty-two thousand Einherjar and physically carrying each and every one of them through the portal and setting them on the field of Utgard. It was like a nightmarish game of Risk, each token a large, smelly Norseman. The hours became days, and the days fell away into weeks. I slept, I think. I must have at some point.

Finally, after eternity had come and passed a few times, I stood on the field before Utgard and looked about me. Standing in a ragged formation were the warriors of Asgard. Looking at the high walls of Utgard, I could just make out the forms of the Giants inside on the parapet. *By every god that was or ever will be, aren't they going to be surprised*, I thought maliciously.

I was in the middle of turning my attention back to the portal to allow time to resume its normal clip when a thought bubble floated to the surface of my mind and popped.

Why didn't you just have Odin open the portal and then march right in there and kill the whole bunch of them instead of hauling a couple million tons of Norsemen through that fucking thing?

All the air shot out of me like I had been gut-punched. My legs gave out and I sat down with an audible *thump*. Holding my head in my hands, I started rocking back and forth, howling with laughter. I laughed so hard tears rolled down my face and I could barely breathe. I don't know how long I sat that way, but I must have started losing focus on time, because I noticed that the Einherjar were beginning to move sluggishly. Wiping my face, I stood and concentrated on the portal. I yelled through it to the Asgardians on the other side to come through. Time began to move normally, and through the portal stepped the gods. *I will be damned if I ever say anything about this to them,* I thought. *And if they know what's good for 'em, they'll never mention it if it occurs to them, either.*

Suddenly, exhaustion washed over me and I could feel myself tottering. Vaguely, I could hear the cacophony of war cries from the Einherjar as they charged the gates of Utgard. My vision tunneled, and I felt myself falling bonelessly forward.

Heimdall was there, however, and caught me in his huge arms like I was no bigger than a child's teddy bear. As my eyes closed, I heard Odin's voice, a thousand miles away, floating from the void.

"Away with him, Heimdall. Move him safely out of the fight. I'll see you in the citadel."

Then darkness took me in and I knew nothing more.

Chapter Seventeen

Consciousness came to in stages. Sounds came to me first, sounding as if the entire world was wrapped in cotton. Then they became clearer, and I could make out individual voices in the background of white noise. When I opened my eyes and felt a million tiny daggers bore into my skull. With a hiss of pain, Instantly, I snapped my eyelids shut again and lay very, very still. Sometime later a hard, calloused hand slipped behind my neck with surprising gentleness and raised my head. A cup was brought to my lips and I drank greedily.

It was on the third of fourth drink of the liquid before I became aware it was mead. I shot through the gamut of intoxication at an incredible speed. In the space of seconds, I went from dead sober to blown in the ditch line and then to a warm, healthy glow. Opening my eyes again, I found myself looking into the eyes of Heimdall, who was looking down at me with a proud, satisfied smile.

My pain and exhaustion slipping away from me like an old blanket, I sat up and looked around me. I was still outside the gates of Utgard, but the citadel had seen better days. Smoke billowed up from several places, and I could hear the crackle of fire. Huge bodies lay all around, twisted into whatever shape death had found them in. Looking back to Heimdall I said, "I take it we won?"

He laughed. "Oh, yes Alexei, we won. Quite handily, as a matter of fact." He helped me to my feet and waved a hand towards the battered gates. "The Allfather would like you to come inside, if you feel able."

I nodded. The mead had returned my strength, and I felt as fresh as a daisy. We began walking towards Utgard. "So, Loki has been re-fettered, then? He and Fenrir?" I asked. Heimdall's face screwed up in a look of angry disgust. I felt a ball of tension in the pit of my stomach. "What happened? What's wrong, Heimdall?"

He just shook his shaggy head and nodded towards the hall before us. When he spoke, his voice was tense and angry. "Loki and Fenrir remain free, Alexei. They were not here when we sprang our trap. *Why* they were not is something the Allfather is currently trying to find out. That is why he has asked for you. Utgard-Loki, King of the Giants, is not being very forthcoming. The Allfather thought that perhaps you might use your… um… *talents* to find out."

The restorative power of the mead seemed to fade away in a flood. Once again, I felt old and worn out. "God-*damn* it", I said, my voice breaking. "All of that for *nothing?!?*"

Heimdall shot me a look. "No, Alexei, it was not for

'*nothing*', as you put it. We were able to take the Citadel of Utgard and decimate countless numbers of our enemies this day. Enemies that we would have had to face at Ragnarok that we no longer have to face. Hundreds of foes fell before our blades. No one can remember such a one-sided victory as the one we enjoyed here today. Loki, wherever he and Fenrir are, can no longer look to Jotunheim for support. Utgard-Loki's armies have been destroyed. He will never regain his strength. Those of his people that remain will never look upon him as a leader again, because he was unable to stop this assault. Loyalty is not highly regarded among the residents of Jotunheim."

"Yeah, I guess so. It's just… well, *dammit*, Heimdall, I thought this would be the end of all this, you know?"

Heimdall's voice was heavy when he replied. "Yes, little brother, I know." For the first time I noticed the blood covering Heimdall's armor and face. Pointing at it, I asked, "Is any of that yours?"

He smiled wanly. "Some of it, little brother. Worry not, I will heal."

That got me thinking. "The rest? The Einherjar? How many did we lose? What happened when they fell? Are they in Valhalla?"

Heimdall's face closed with an almost audible snap. His voice was steely. "We lost just over two thousand Einherjar. As to what happened to them when they fell…" He pointed across the vast courtyard, where men were lining the bodies of the fallen up against the wall. Blood covered the limp bodies, and they rolled bonelessly as the surviving Einherjar moved them reverently into position. Aghast, I looked at Heimdall. He looked forward, still walking purposefully toward the great hall. His voice was soft but without false hope.

"They remain as they fell, Alexei. If they were going to return to Valhalla, their bodies would have done so when they died. They have not. Thus, we know that they have not returned to Valhalla. Emissaries have been dispatched to see if they have perhaps wound up under the supervision of Hel, Queen of the Dead. The emissaries have not yet returned." He blew out a pent-up breath. "I know not, little brother. Here lie their bodies. You see them as I do. But where are their souls?" He shook his head helplessly. "That, I cannot say. But come, let us not keep the Allfather waiting. Perhaps with your help, Utgard-Loki will be more... disposed, shall we say, to helping us find that pig-spawn son of a whore and end this farce." He turned to me and gripped my shoulder. "Be of good heart, Alexei. Our brothers shall not have fallen in vain, no matter where their souls now reside." He began walking again, and I fell into step beside him. *Yes*, I thought, *this son of a bitch will be more disposed. Greatly so. These men deserve nothing less.*

With this thought pounding in my head, Heimdall and I entered the hall of Utgard-Loki, King of the Giants. We walked down the length of the hall, it too bearing the marks of recent violence. At the end of the hall was a massive throne and sitting upon it was Utgard-Loki, the king of Jotunheim. He sat perfectly still, not a muscle moving. He had good reason for this, as Odin's spear, Gungnir, rested its tip at his throat. The

Allfather stood almost as still as the failed king, one finger tapping against the shaft of his spear. He turned his head and nodded at us when he heard our entry. Turning his single ice-blue eye back to Utgard-Loki, he said, "May I introduce my son, your Highness? Heimdall you know already. The man beside him is my mortal son, Alexei Addison. It is through his good graces that my Einherjar were able to arrive at your gate this day. Alexei, this is Utgard-Loki, King of Jotunheim."

I nodded at him and received a murderous look in return. When he spoke, his voice dripped hatred. "You are the reason so many of mine lie dead in their own halls, having brought harm to none? You have visited this abomination on my people? Alexei Addison, is it? A name that will be long remembered in Jotunheim, I assure you. You have slept your last peaceful night... you and yours. This, I swear to you."

Odin growled and edged the spear a few millimeters closer to the king's throat. I motioned for him to back off, which he did. This seemed to surprise Utgard-Loki, and the king looked at me closely. Now that I had his undivided attention, I spoke to him for the first time.

"Yes, it was I that brought the Einherjar to your gates. However, you can quit with the 'Oh, poor, pitiful, peace-loving us' bullshit. I would not have brought an army to your door had you not made a deal with Loki. You know it, and so do I."

His eyes widened slightly at this revelation, but that was it. I had to hand it to him; he had guts, if nothing else. In a flat voice, he said, "I know nothing of this thing you speak. The actions of Loki are not my concern, nor the concern of my people. You have brought illegal warfare to my realm, and I will see you pay for it."

I shook my head. "First off, your Highness, I shouldn't have to point this out, but you're not exactly in a position to be throwing threats around. You keep acting like Captain Bad-Ass, and I doubt somewhat seriously that you'll 'see' me do anything at all, let alone 'pay'. Your army is crushed; your citadel is in the hands of your enemies. What is to keep us from destroying everything we find, and putting every living creature in all of Jotunheim to the sword?"

Utgard-Loki drew a hissed breath, and I could see Odin open his mouth to deny what I was saying. I made a slight motion to him, hoping he would see it and let me play this out. Heimdall saw, and must have seen where I was going, because he said, "You know, Allfather, Alexei may well be right. This could be the perfect opportunity for us to end forever the threat of Jotunheim. Ragnarok will be a much easier fight without the legions of Utgard-Loki against us."

Odin looked from Heimdall to me and back again. I never took my eyes off of Utgard-Loki. If the Allfather wanted me to get some information from the defeated Giant in front of me, he was going to have to let me run this bluff out. Finally, Odin spoke, his voice heavy with regret. "I suppose there is some merit in this, Alexei. It is not the way of Asgard to butcher those who cannot defend themselves, but... yes, I suppose there is something to be said for your logic. This business with Loki has changed all the rules, has it not?"

Utgard-Loki was now breathing in shallow pants. His voice was full of disbelief when he said, "*You*, Allfather? You would give your blessing to the slaughter of women and children, the old and infirm? Is this what passes for honor in Asgard now?" He took a deep breath and then laughed. Yes, there was no shortage of guts in the creature, I had to admit. "Fine, O honorable and great Asgardians. Ravage the length and breadth of Jotunheim, killing at will. How many more of your Einherjar will fall in that endeavor? Think you that the battle this day was vicious? Once words spreads that you are following a policy of genocide, all of Jotunheim will rise against you. At each pass, at each mountain fastness, you will see your army bleed. You may well succeed in the end, but at what cost? I have seen the bodies of your warriors lying dead before me. You will not have them to stand at your side come Ragnarok. We will bleed you dry, *one man at a time*!!!" Having spoken, Utgard-Loki fell back against his throne, defiance shining in his eyes.

I came forward until we were only a few feet apart. Looking into his eyes, I gave him the most horrible smile I could manage. It must have been a fairly bad one, because he recoiled in confusion. Still smiling, I said, "Yes, your Highness, what you say is true. Such a campaign would be costly. Of course, such a thing would have no reason to occur, should you simply answer a few questions concerning your dealings with Loki. Is that so much to ask? We offer your kingdom and the lives of your subjects for a little information. That strikes me as a bargain. What do you say?"

I could tell that my words had the effect on him that I had hoped for. He laughed in my face and turned his head to address Odin. "Is this the best your loins can produce now, Allfather?" Odin's knuckles turned white on the shaft of his spear. Utgard-Loki seemed to dismiss me from his sight. "Pah, strike, Asgardian. I have no more patience for such womanly behavior. Strike and be damned to the lot of you. You will run out of wood for the funeral pyres long before you leave the boundaries of Jotunheim." He made a flicking motion with his fingers and for a second I was afraid that Odin was going to grant him his wish. The tip of the spear wavered minutely in front of Utgard-Loki's throat.

To forestall this, I said blandly, "Very well. Allfather, kill this creature as you will. I will begin the ritual."

Utgard-Loki's face changed from defiant to confused and concerned instantly. "What ritual do you speak of, half-blood? I suppose you have some great power brought from Midgard, hmm?"

I turned to him and said simply, "Yes. I do. Would you like to see an example of what awaits your people, Your Highness?"

Still looking confused, Utgard-Loki said, "Certainly. Astound me with your limitless powers. I was unaware that Midgard produced such."

I turned half away from Utgard-Loki and gave Odin and Heimdall a look that screamed "I hope this works", and then centered myself. It was getting easier to tap into that odd blue light that seemed to flood my body from my core. Within seconds, my arms were covered with throbbing blue light. Picking a giant's corpse, I sent wave after wave of the light into it. The corpse shuddered and withered in seconds. I let the light die. Where the body of a giant had been there was nothing but a pile of ashes, which were whipped away in the breeze that blew through the open door of the hall.

I heard a pained gasp from Utgard-Loki. I turned and fixed him with an emotionless stare. After a few heavy moments, I said, "Now, King of Jotunheim, you know what I can do. What I did to that corpse was only a small taste of what I can accomplish when I perform the ritual. Speak now of your dealings with Loki, or I will see that you are the last of the Giants alive. You will watch as all of Jotunheim is covered by that killing light." I began to walk back towards him, raising my voice as I went. "I will watch as you see every living creature in Jotunheim falls away into fire! I will make it so every man, woman, and child knows that it was because of the treachery of Utgard-Loki that they die in agony! The last thing that passes the lips of all of Jotunheim will be to curse their fool of a King! Now, SPEAK, YOU WRETCHED SON OF A PIG!!!"

Utgard-Loki fell into himself in front of us. His hands came up like a supplicant. His voice was strained and broken, and he was weeping openly. "Please, Asgardian! I will tell you what you want to know! Only visit not this devastation upon my people!"

I was sick to my stomach. I turned away before Utgard-Loki could see the anguish on my face. I mumbled something to Odin and made my way out of the hall. Heimdall turned and followed me outside. I could hear the low murmur of Odin putting questions to the humbled king of Jotunheim.

I barely made it outside before I lost my lunch. Thor and Tyr were standing nearby, overseeing the funeral pyres of the Einherjar. They raised their eyebrows in question to Heimdall, who shook his head and raised his hand to them. They nodded back, shared a confused look, and returned to their duties. Heimdall placed a strong hand on my shoulder. "It is all right, little brother", he said. "Had you not done what you did, more would have suffered and died, Einherjar and Giants both. You have saved lives this day."

I raised myself back up to a standing position, the back of my throat still stinging with acidic vomit. When I could finally speak, I managed to husk out "Yeah, I guess so, Heimdall. I'm just not cut out for this whole 'I'll murder your entire population' thing, even if I was only bluffing."

Heimdall gave me an odd look. When he spoke, his voice was quiet. "Are you sure you *were* bluffing? How do you know that you cannot do just as you threatened to do? You have no idea the limits of your power by your own admission. You might well have been capable of sending that killing light over Jotunheim. And believe me, little brother, there are those in Asgard… in *many* realms… that would think you not only right for doing it, but call you a hero and treat you as a king."

My look of horror must have been answer enough for Heimdall, because he smiled and said to me, "I know that you cannot do that, even if your power allowed you to. You have too much honor. For this, I am glad. Although I have no love for the inhabitants of Jotunheim, neither do I wish to see an entire race eradicated. Such is beneath me, and I am glad to see it beneath you as well."

I could only stand with my mouth hanging open. Murder an entire people? Even if they weren't *people*, technically speaking? Visions of that damned blue light pulsing out from my hands and killing every living thing in Jotunheim shot through my mind, and I once again doubled over, retching.

Heimdall stood patiently by my side, his hand a comforting weight on my back. Thor walked over and asked what was wrong with me. Heimdall filled him in on what had gone on in the throne room. Tyr walked over at some point in the narrative and cast a speculative eye towards me. When he spoke, his voice was calm and matter-of-fact. "Could you do it, Alexei? I mean, cast morality or honor aside for a moment. I mean, do you think you could physically do what you threatened Utgard-Loki you would do? Is your power as strong as that?"

I looked helplessly at the men around me. I couldn't keep the quaver out my voice when I answered. "I have no idea, guys. Look, a week ago I was a college student, okay? Since then, I've learned that Odin is my dad, all the Norse myths are true, that the craziest one of those myths would like to see me dead and gone, and that I can shoot some sort of blue light out of me that either kills or cures. It's a bit much to take in, all right? So, no, Tyr, I don't know if I could destroy Jotunheim with my super-nifty ray gun. Maybe I could, but I will goddamned if I *will*!"

From behind me came Odin's voice. "I am glad to hear that you would not, Alexei, but I do not appreciate your blasphemy."

I whipped my head around and felt my eyes bulge. "My *what*?!?"

"Your blasphemy", Odin replied calmly. "You said 'goddamned'." He curled his lip in distaste as he said the last word.

Well, I was now officially over the high side, mentally speaking. My voice rang with incredulity and rage when I spoke. "Hold the phone, just hold the damn phone here a second." I could sense Heimdall, Thor, and Tyr tense beside me. They obviously were *not* accustomed to anyone addressing the Allfather in that tone. Well, *fuck* them. "Do you mean to tell me that after we killed so many people that we're literally covered in blood that you're gonna jump my ass for using the Lord's name in vain? The *Christian* Lord?" This last had sarcasm dripping from each word.

Odin was unfazed by my demeanor. His voice still calm, he said, "All gods deserve respect, regardless of what gods they are. I would no more tolerate blasphemy directed at Allah than at Jehovah. You must remember your place in this universe, Alexei. There is no place for scorn for those greater than you. Remember that. You are not so grand that you can scoff at god. *Any* god."

I threw my hands into the air in disgust. "Fine. Sorry. I'll just hop off to the nearest church and ask for forgiveness, shall I?"

Odin's single eye blazed out, and for a moment I thought I had seriously screwed up. Having the

Allfather angry at you is an unpleasant place to be, trust me.

Odin spoke again, his voice pitched low and deadly. "You will find time enough to ask forgiveness at a later date. Now, my *son*, if it would not trouble you over- much, shall we leave this place and act upon the information Utgard-Loki was so willing to give, or shall we wait until you have found your church?"

I couldn't meet his gaze and dropped my eyes to my boot tops. I mumbled something about being ready if everyone else was. Odin spun on his heel and began to bark orders to prepare to leave. When he had been gone for several minutes, I finally found the strength to raise my eyes. Thor was looking at me with open hostility, Tyr with marked distain, and Heimdall with sad, pitying eyes. Thor turned around with a growl and went off to help the Allfather prepare to leave, and Tyr followed. Heimdall stood where he had been the whole time, his massive arms crossed. Finally, when I couldn't stand it any longer, I blurted, "What? Why was the Allfather so pissed at me?"

Heimdall reached out and grasped my shoulder. "Do you remember when you first met me and we went to your dorm room?"

I was taken aback. "Well, yeah, Heimdall, I remember. Having a giant Norse god show up at your dorm isn't something a person is likely to forget quickly. Why?"

"Do you remember the poster on your wall of Thor?"

I looked at him blankly for a moment and then said, "Oh, yeah, the one about the cross and the nails? Yeah. What about it?"

"Do you further remember what I said about that poster?"

"Yes, I remember. You said something about the Allfather ripping the damned thing down and making me eat it, and that he was pretty hardcore about religion. Okay, I can see you weren't joking, but I gotta ask… what is the *deal* with that?"

Heimdall looked off into the distance. His voice was strained when he answered. "The Allfather knows firsthand, as we all do, what it means to lose the faith of humanity. I have told you of our existence here, living in the half-light of eternity. Unable to live as we did when mankind worshipped us, unable to fade away into the universal dust from which we came. It is not a particularly pleasant sensation, Alexei. Our lives, our existence, means nothing to mankind anymore, therefore *we* mean nothing to mankind. Our every action means nothing. Our victories, our defeats, our love, our hatred…nothing. The Allfather cannot stand to see any religion belittled, no matter what it may be. He would not wish that fate on any god. Do you understand now why he is so touchy about the subject?"

I stood silently for a moment, ingesting what Heimdall had said. Finally, I spoke. "I am sorry, Heimdall. I didn't understand. But in my own defense, how could I? I don't know what it means to be a god, so I can't really be expected to understand what it feels like to be one, forgotten or otherwise. You dig what I'm saying? I meant no offense."

Heimdall turned to me, his eyes a bit harder than I was used to seeing. His voice held a slight edge to it. "It is not to me you should be making this apology, Alexei." He jerked his thumb over his shoulder towards where Odin was finishing up preparations for departure.

"Okay, I can take a hint, Mr. Subtle", I said. "I'll go talk to him."

Heimdall simply nodded and went back to studying the horizon as if there was something very interesting there. Hell, for him, maybe there was. The ability to see and hear almost everything was a great gift, but it was most likely a major pain in the ass sometimes as well.

I trudged over to where Odin and the others were finishing up things in the courtyard. The bodies of the fallen Einherjar were now ash, and there armor and weapons stood in piles in neat rows. I thought about what would happen to these objects once we departed Jotunheim and shuddered. Odin noticed and asked what was wrong.

"When we leave, won't the Giants desecrate these monuments?"

Odin smiled grimly. He turned to me and said, "Do you really think so? After the exhibition you gave Utgard-Loki? No, Alexei, these things we leave behind will be as safe here as they would be in Valhalla. None of the Giants are brave enough to so much as approach them. After we have finished our business with Loki and Fenrir, we will return for them and give them a place of honor in Asgard."

I was thankful that Odin was speaking to me without the undertone of disgust I had heard earlier, and I jumped on the opportunity to tell him what I had told Heimdall. He stood silently for what seemed to be a very long time before he finally spoke. "Alexei, perhaps I was wrong to have been so harsh with you. You are correct, you are a man, and as such, cannot be expected to understand all that we are. So, perhaps we both erred. I am willing to let this go if you are. However, in the future, will you refrain from using blasphemous phrases around me? Out of respect, perhaps?"

I stuck my hand out and the Allfather grasped it firmly. I looked him directly in his single eye and said, "I will do so, Father. Should I say anything blasphemous around you, please understand that it is an accident, and that I mean nothing by it. In my world, I am very used to doing so. Knowing what I know now, I am not so inclined."

Odin smiled at me, his eye bright. "Well spoken, my son. And it does my heart good to hear that word from your lips."

I smiled back, confused. "Which word was that?"

Odin kept right on smiling. "Father."

I couldn't help but smile back.

Chapter Eighteen

Our return journey from Jotunheim held none of the boisterousness that our trip in had. Our losses had been comparatively light, but the fact that the fallen Einherjar had not returned to Valhalla weighed heavily on all our hearts and minds. It seemed that with Loki's freedom, all the known rules had been thrown to the wind. Odin had opened a portal and called the horses to us, so we were returning the old-fashioned way. I had *no* problem with that, I assure you.

I looked back down the line of men and took sad note at the rider-less horses that trudged along, seeming to feel the loss of their riders even as we did. I felt the stone against my heart grow heavier and nearly wept aloud. I couldn't allow myself to do so in front of these grim, brave men, however, so I shoved the tears back and focused on the road in front of me. We had traveled for quite some time before a thought struck me. I turned to Heimdall, who was riding beside me. Thor was still angry at my treatment of Odin earlier, and was several places in front of me, and hadn't spoken since we left Jotunheim. Looking at Heimdall, I said,

"You told me that once, when man worshipped you, the Einherjar would battle each day, only to revive with the coming of night to feast, and then they would do it all over again the next day, right?"

Heimdall lifted an eyebrow at me. "Yes, that was how it was when man worshipped the Aesir. Why do you ask what you already know?"

I thought hard for a moment. Finally, I asked, "How many people have to worship you to make things as they were before?"

He seemed taken aback by the question. He scratched his beard reflectively. "Truth be told, Alexei, I have no idea. There is no set number, I think. It could take thousands, or it could take only one. But again, why?"

I began to grow excited. "There are people that worship the Norse pantheon on Midgard now", I said, my voice happy. "It's called Astratu, or something like that. I saw it on the Internet. They have churches and everything. There's your answer! Surely whole churches of people should be enough to bring back the old ways, right?"

Heimdall smiled sadly and looked around. "Does it seem to you that these people are enough to bring back our glory?"

Damn him, he had a point. Asgard remained as it had been, drenched in eternal half-light and snowy gloom. When he spoke again, his voice was kind, but sad.

"I have seen these people that you speak of, Alexei. Remember? That's what I do. They call out to us, but they have patterned themselves, or have been influenced, too much by Christianity to bring our glory back. They mean well, but they are not Norse, though they may call themselves so."

"Dammit", I mumbled. "I thought that might work."

"You thought what might work, little brother?"

"I thought that, if the Astratu, or whatever, could bring back your glory, then when the sun shone again on Asgard, the fallen Einherjar would return to their place in Valhalla."

Heimdall was again contemplative. "Yes, I see what you mean", he said, "but I don't think we should count on that, seeing as things are as they have been for almost a thousand years."

I looked out over the snow-covered evening that was forever here. Suddenly, a thought shot through my mind like a meteor. In my excitement, I grabbed Heimdall by the arm. My motion caused both our mounts to stop, and the Einherjar behind us had to pull up short. Pulling his horse's head to one side, Heimdall led us both off the path so the rest of the company could move on. Once clear of the path, Heimdall looked at me quizzically. "What ails you, little brother?"

"Nothing ails me, Heimdall", I nearly shouted, "Not one damn thing ails me at all! And soon, nothing will ail the men we lost, either!"

Heimdall flicked a glance at the passing men, who

were looking at us in confusion. "Lower your voice", he hissed at me. "These men have lost brothers, and your false hope will do them no good!"

I shook my head. "But that's just it! It isn't false hope! Once all this is done and we have re-fettered Loki and Fenrir, I'll go back home, right?"

Heimdall continued to look confused. "Of course you will. Once your service here is complete, you will return to your home. Midgard is yours; we would not expect you to remain here in this half-life with us."

"Exactly! And when I get back, do you know what I'm gonna do?"

Now Heimdall was beginning to look a little put out and impatient. "I know not", he said, "bed the first wench you find?"

"No, you big dumb ass! I'm gonna make an altar, sacrifice a bull, do the fucking chicken dance if I have to, but I'm gonna believe in you all enough to bring the sun back to Asgard! The Einherjar will return! Imagine this place as it was, Heimdall! It will be like it was!"

My excitement seemed to be catching. Heimdall's eyes grew brighter and a huge smile lit up his face. Grabbing me in a bear hug, he nearly squeezed me in half. "Come", he said, "we must tell the Allfather of this! Imagine it, Asgard in its glory..." his voice trailed off and then I suddenly found myself flying like a bat out of hell along the path. Heimdall had both my reins and his own, and he wasn't letting any grass grow under us, believe me. The Einherjar, having ridden past us, now found themselves trying desperately to get out of our way.

Odin and Thor were at the head of the column, talking about something. Hearing the ruckus behind them, they turned in their saddles to see what was going on. Odin raised an eyebrow, but Thor retained his angry expression. Heimdall either didn't see it, or didn't take note of it. *I* did, however. I was still on Thor's shit-list in a big way, and he wasn't about to let me forget it.

Heimdall was slightly out of breath when he spoke. "Allfather, you must hear what Alexei has to say!"

"Does he?" asked Thor. "And why must he do that? Has my young *half*-brother some more tripe to disrespect our father with?"

Okay, enough was enough. Odin and I were fine, as he had let me know in the courtyard in Jotunheim. Thor obviously hadn't gotten that particular memo.

"Enough, Thor", I said, my voice cold. "I have made my apologies to the Allfather, and he has accepted. I made a mistake, and I have admitted it." I could see Thor bristling, and he placed a hand on his hammer. With the meanest look I could muster, I said, "You need another lesson, big brother?" I let that set in for a minute and was shocked to see that *yes*, by god, he *did* want another lesson.

I shook my head in aggravation. I was setting myself to go at it again with the Thunder God when Heimdall broke in. "Stay your hand, you fool! Listen to what Alexei has to say!"

Well, I guess being called a fool wasn't high on Thor's list of favorite things, but be damned if he wasn't about to take Heimdall and me on at the same time. Points for guts, but minus several for intelligence. It seemed like things were about to get really exciting for a second when Odin raised his hand and said in a flat, declarative voice, "Thor, enough. I have warned you time and again about your temper and the trouble it gets you in. I grow weary of it."

Now Thor looked positively crushed. "So, you take their side against me as well, Father? Am I to stand alone in this matter? This… *human*", here he flung a contemptuous hand in my direction, "gave offence to you. Now I, who would stand for your honor, am called down as a child would be? What justice is this?"

Odin turned his head to look Thor directly in the face. When he spoke, his voice was softer. "Thor, I love you much. You are my son and often give me great joy and pride. But you must *think* before you act, my son. Alexei has in fact apologized to me, and I have accepted. In fact, I apologized to him, as well, for I was in the wrong as much as he."

Great, Dad, I thought, *did you really have to tell him that?*

Thor looked aghast at Odin. "You apologized to *him*??? In the name of all we stand for, *why*??? Why would you abase yourself so?"

I decided that I needed to step in. Maybe this wasn't my place, but I could see things from Thor's eyes. He was only trying to defend his father's honor, something that I could completely understand. I spoke to him gently. "Thor, the Allfather did apologize to me, although I neither asked for it, nor do I feel I deserved it. We had a disagreement. That's all. I was out of line, and I spoke in anger, without thinking. But have you not told me that you suffer from this same problem from time to time? Can I not be forgiven my foolish behavior, or am I *that* beneath you? You called me brother, and told me that you would stand at my side. Has that changed because I spoke without thinking?"

I knew I was hitting him where it hurt the most, because his temper was his greatest shame to him. He looked down for a moment, and then shook himself all over like a huge dog. When he raised his head to look at me, some of the fire was gone from his eyes. "You speak the truth, Alexei. I have been forgiven countless times because of my foolishness. I suppose I should grant you the same forgiveness."

He reached his hand out to clasp mine. I took it, prepared for a repeat of our first meeting, but he was content to crush my hand a little and then release me. He looked over at Heimdall, who was practically dancing in agitation to speak. "Now, what was it you had to say to the Allfather, Alexei?"

I started to speak, but Heimdall was far too excited and overrode me. He was nearly finished explaining everything to Odin when the Allfather began shaking his head sadly.

I looked at Heimdall and saw the confusion in my face mirrored in his. He looked back at Odin and asked, "What is it? Why do you shake your head so?"

Heimdall had asked the question, but Odin chose to

answer me. "Alexei, what is faith?" he asked.

I was flummoxed. I was totally unprepared for the question and began stammering. Odin raised his hand for silence. "Let me ask it another way. Look to your steed."

I did. "Okay, I see my horse, but I still don't understand."

Odin nodded, as if this was just what he had expected. "You see your horse. It is there, holding you up, yes?" I nodded, still confused. "You see your horse, so you know your horse is there. Now, what if you could no longer see it? Would you remain where you are, in midair, or would you fall to the ground?"

What the *hell?* Invisible horses? Say what you will, but Odin could sure go the long way around to make a point. After a moment, I said cautiously, "I suppose if I couldn't see it, but it was still there, I would stay where I am. If I couldn't see it because it *wasn't* there, I'd be on my ass on the ground…uh…wouldn't I?"

Odin nodded and smiled. "Exactly. If the horse was not there, you would fall. But you know the horse *is* there, because you can see it. You need no *faith* in the horse, because it is something you can see and feel and touch. If someone asked you to mount a horse you could not see, you would need *faith* that it was there in order to consider mounting it, yes?"

Thor looked positively befuddled, but the light of comprehension began to shine in Heimdall's eyes. A second later, it hit me, as well. I let out a groan. "You mean that when this is all over and I go back home it won't matter what I do, don't you?" I asked. "I could build the biggest monument to Asgard ever built and the sun wouldn't shine one bit here… all because I've *seen* you all, and I *know* you're here. I *know* you're real."

Again Odin nodded. "Faith is the belief in that which we cannot see, Alexei. Your faith in us is unnecessary, because you stand before us. You believe in us, but faith is something different altogether."

I let out a sigh of defeat. "I thought I could fix it", I said. "I really thought I could bring them all back." Although I tried to stop it, a single tear made its way down my face. Thor seemed shocked to see a grown man cry, and Heimdall seemed as dejected as I was. Odin placed a hand on my shoulder.

"My son, your hope is a testament to the love you feel for the men that stand by your side. There is no shame in the tear you shed." He gripped my shoulder harder for a moment, and then let go. When he spoke again, his voice was icy, all the warmth from a moment ago gone. "What we shall do to honor those that have fallen from our ranks and those innocents that have fallen on Midgard is to find Loki and Fenrir, and place them back where they belong. This time, however, I think that their suffering shall increase a thousand fold."

I had experienced a fair amount of fear since Heimdall had made his first appearance at my dorm, but nothing up to that point had prepared me for the wrath that fell from that single eye. I suddenly found myself very, very glad I was not Loki or Fenrir. Deciding to grab the bull by the horns, I asked, "How are we going to capture Loki and Fenrir? Did Utgard-Loki give you any information about them?"

Odin gave me a grim smile. "Oh, yes, Utgard-Loki was *very* forthcoming about all he knew, although in retrospect, it seems foolish of me not having thought of it myself."

We asked him what he meant, but he refused to say anything more until we reached Valhalla. Seeing that he was sincere, we then put our steeds back in motion and moved on at full speed.

We arrived soon after our conversation on the road and went into the vast Hall to discuss our next move. The Einherjar went about seeing to the horses and checking their weapons, re-sharpening those that had been dulled on Giant bones and Giant flesh. Walking to the head of the massive table, Odin sat down on his throne. His wolves curled up to his feet, and almost as if on cue, his ravens flew in and landed on his shoulders. The raven on his left shoulder began to caw and shriek, but Odin merely sat as if listening to a report. After a few moments of this, the raven fell silent. Odin shook his head with a sigh and then gazed at each of us in turn. His voice was heavy with grief when he said, "Huginn has been to the realm of Hel, and the fallen Einherjar are not there. He says that Hel herself seemed quite satisfied that her father was creating such chaos." He shook himself and said, "Well, we must carry on. We owe them no less."

We all stood, looking expectantly at the Allfather, waiting to hear what news he had gotten from Utgard-Loki. He laid his hands out on the table and began to speak.

"It makes me angry with myself that I haven't been able to figure out Loki's plans more quickly, especially when he freed Fenrir. By doing so, he has hastened what hopes to be the coming of Ragnarok. Although Huginn could find no trace, it would not surprise me if Loki has been, or will be, entering Hel to speak with his daughter. Utgard-Loki told me that Loki promised him that he would soon be in possession of Naglfar, and would bring the Giants into Asgard."

Aside to Heimdall, I asked, "What the hell is Naglfar?" However, Odin heard me and answered me himself.

"Naglfar is a boat made from dead men's nails that is to carry the Giants here when Ragnarok begins." I couldn't suppress a shudder, at which Odin grinned. "Yes, my son, it is as horrid in reality as your mind is telling you. The dead men that will supply these nails are to be found in Hel, so it is only reasonable that Loki must go there."

Thor's hand tightened around the handle of Mjollnir. Hatred dripped like venom from his every word. "Then it is to Hel we are bound, and woe unto Loki if he be foolish enough to be there when we arrive."

Odin held up a hand. "You forget something, Thor. Loki wishes to bring forth Ragnarok now; do not all things point toward this?"

We all nodded. It did seem to be the madman's goal.

"Very well, then. If it is Ragnarok Loki seeks, as his

actions make clear, then isn't there something else he must do before boarding Naglfar for his trip here?"

There was a pensive moment as each of us looked at each other. I, for one, had no frigging clue what else was required to kick-start the end of time. After a moment, Heimdall gave a small gasp. His shocked face turned to Odin and he said, "Surely not, Allfather! But... I suppose..."

Thor still looked lost at sea, but Odin was nodding. "Yes, my sons, Loki has one other destination and purpose before boarding his accursed boat. His children are all free, with the exception of..." He let the question hang in the air like a scythe blade.

Suddenly, Thor gave a convulsive jerk that sent platters and silverware flying. I barely dodged out of the way of a particularly menacing-looking fork as it shot past me. Thor lurched to his feet and roared. I was still in the dark, but it was painfully obvious that *something* had seriously pissed the giant man off. I looked nervously at Heimdall, who shrugged in a helpless way. He opened his mouth to explain what was going on when Thor found his ability to speak.

"That son of a misbegotten WHORE!!! He would *dare*??? He truly has gone mad, then. So be it! If it is his wish to unleash that abomination, then I stand ready to destroy it!"

I was still a little uneasy, but I figured that something that could elicit that sort of reaction from Thor might be something I needed to know about. So, I girded my loins for the expected explosion and asked, "What abomination would that be, Thor?"

The Thunder God spun around to face me. His red hair had electricity crackling up and down it, and his eyes were absolutely terrifying. In a booming voice, he roared, "What abomination? *I'll* tell you what abomination! That psychotic, crazy-eyed, crippled, thrice-bedamned..." Thor sputtered, at a loss for words, so I gave him a hand.

"Motherfucker?" I supplied. *Well, so much for the obscenity rule.*

His eyes lit up. "YES!!!! MOTHERFUCKER!!! That psychotic, crazy-eyed, crippled, thrice-damned MOTHERFUCKER is going to try to free Jormungand, that's what he's going to do!" He fell back in his seat, breathing like a bull. A really, really *big* bull.

Once again I found myself wishing that I had paid closer attention in class when we had covered Norse mythology. I gritted my teeth and said in the most polite voice I could manage, "And Jormungand would be *who*, exactly?"

Thor looked at me like I had just pissed in his mother's face, not an expression I found helpful. Odin said warningly, "Thor..." and Heimdall moved a bit closer to me. *This does not bode well*, I thought. *Maybe I should go see if the Einherjar need any help with the horses...*

Much to my relief, Thor slumped back into his seat, mumbling about how ignorant mankind had become. I chose, wisely I thought, to ignore this and give my full attention to Odin. After glancing at Thor to ensure he wasn't about to try and fry me again, Odin looked back at me.

"You know, Alexei, while Thor may be a bit short on manners, he has a point. All this has been passed down among your kind. You should have at least *some* knowledge of our history."

"Or maybe just a damned library card", Thor mumbled darkly.

I threw my hands up in supplication. "I know, I know. I'm sorry. I should know all this stuff. But try to remember guys, I am studying to be a *lawyer*, and there isn't a huge need for knowledge about Norse mythology on the Bar exam, from what I've heard."

Thor didn't seem especially mollified by this explanation, but it seemed to suit Odin. He gave me one last exasperated look and then explained.

"Jormungand is also known as the Midgard Serpent. He is the offspring of Loki and the Giantess Angrboda. Incidentally, Angrboda is also the mother of Fenrir and Hel. And stop referring us as 'mythology', if you don't mind."

I couldn't help myself. I really couldn't. "Jeez, guys, didn't any of you talk to Loki about practicing safe sex?"

After about ten minutes, things had settled down enough for the conversation to continue. The chair behind me was scorched by a huge lightning bolt, and Heimdall's chain-mail had gotten red hot, causing him to jerk it off and fling it to the floor, where it was currently cracking and popping as it cooled off. Heimdall gave me a dark look. Well, I didn't ask him to sit so close to me, dammit. My ever-present blue glow had kept me completely unharmed, but I was getting murderous glances from everyone in the room. I thought it was time for a tactical apology.

"I am really, *really* sorry, all of you. I didn't mean anything by it; it's just something that happens when I get nervous; I run off at the mouth. I honestly didn't mean to piss anyone off."

Well, that didn't exactly cause everyone to wrap me in a big family hug, but no one tried to kill me, either, so I called it a win.

Odin didn't look angry, just disappointed. Oddly enough, I would rather he had been pissed at me. He looked from Thor to me and back again. Finally, he muttered, "It must run on *my* side of the family, because they have different mothers…" Looking back at me, he said, "You and Thor are very much alike in at least one aspect Alexei: neither of you seems to be able to stop your mouth from running when your wits are asleep."

Zing. That one hurt, but I deserved it. Putting on my most pious face, I asked, "Would someone please tell me who Jormungand is, and why Thor is so angry about it? I apologize again for my lack of knowledge, but I honestly don't know what is so bad about this."

Odin took up the thread of the story, since Thor would not even look my way. Heimdall was just about as pissed at me as Thor, really. *Making friends everywhere you go, Addison,* I thought, *you da man.*

"Jormungand, or the Midgard Serpent, surrounds Midgard. *All* of Midgard. That should give you a bit of an idea just how large it is."

I gave Odin my patented eye-popping stare. "You mean to tell me that there is a snake that encircles the entire planet and no one has *noticed* it??? I find that a little hard to swallow, fellas."

Heimdall answered, his anger still *very* apparent. "Really? And I suppose there wasn't a giant rainbow bridge that landed in the University of Kentucky football field that brought you to Asgard, and you didn't just come back from a battle with Giants, and…"

I held my hands up. "Okay, okay, I get it. You win. It's just… I mean… well, we've got submarines and stuff like that, so I just sort of figured something that huge would have been noticed by now, that's all. Sorry." It seemed like my apology-tank was going to run dry at this rate.

Odin clapped his hands, just once. "Gentlemen, if you please. We have a great deal of work ahead of us, and this foolishness is simply wasting time we do not have."

Properly chastised, we all turned out attention back to the Allfather.

"Now", he continued as if nothing had happened, "in order to get to his son, Loki will have to return to Midgard. This is not something he can do openly, because he knows we are on his trail. So, how will he go about it? Does anyone have any ideas?"

There was silence for a few minutes while we all clapped on our thinking caps. Finally, Heimdall said,

"Loki won't risk traveling between the worlds, not now, not with Tyr on Fenrir's trail. He *could* leave Fenrir behind, I suppose, but that would leave him vulnerable. Plus the fact is, Fenrir is completely insane, and there's no way Loki could be sure that Fenrir would be where he left him once he returned from Midgard. In his current state, Fenrir is just as likely to come charging the gates of Asgard as he is to do anything else. That is just as true in Midgard, so Loki really can't risk taking him there, either. So, if Loki cannot pass over into Midgard, then he needs someone else to do so for him. He *could* have used Baugi, but Fenrir turned him into a snack. So... who else would he send? Who could he trust, and more to the point, who could actually summon Jormungand once they were in Midgard?"

The question was valid, and we all started thinking *hard*. After a few minutes, a thought came to me. I was a little hesitant to voice it, seeing as I was not exactly the most popular person in the room, but I figured what the hell, no one else seemed to have any ideas of their own. Clearing my throat, I said, "Whoever goes after this Jormungand will have to be really, really powerful, right? I mean, it would take someone with immense strength to bring it down."

The Aesir sat looking at me expectantly. After a moment, Odin said, "Yes, Alexei, it would take someone with immense strength. In fact, the only one of the Aesir that can deal with Jormungand is Thor."

Then it hit me like a hammer, no pun intended. During Ragnarok, Thor and the Midgard Serpent were destined to kill one another. No wonder he had been so pissed off at the thought of the thing showing up at his doorstep. I looked over at him. There was still smoke creeping out from under the edges of his helmet. "Damn, Thor, I'm sorry. I didn't realize what that would mean for you if Jormungand were to come to Asgard. Shit, I am *so* sorry."

Thor just flapped a hand at me, but I could tell he wasn't pissed at me anymore. When he spoke, his voice was flat. "My fate is sealed, as is the fate of everyone in this room. I will do what is necessary, and I will die well."

Hearing him say it like that sent a shudder down my spine. It also brought it home to me that this wasn't just about the Einherjar; this was about the gods, too. They would die just the same as the men they shared this hall with. The shudder turned into a stiffening of my spine and I said stoutly, "Well, then, we just won't let it come to that then, will we? We'll keep that snake where it belongs, and then we'll slap Loki and Fenrir in the damned stockade. How's that sound?"

Odin smiled at my forced bravado. "That sounds like a fine plan Alexei, but we must figure out exactly *how* we are going to implement it."

I grinned. "Well, that's what I was gonna say next. Since it would take Thor to get that snake into Asgard, and I *seriously* doubt Loki is gonna ask *him*, what does that leave us with?"

Again, they looked at me expectantly.

"Back home", I began, "believe it or not, I'm considered a big guy. Most folks don't want to mess with me. It's been that way since I was a kid. Once I got to be a teenager, I was quite the town terror for a while. I'd get into meanness, and even the local cops didn't want to mess with me, on account of my size and my sunny disposition."

Odin smiled and said, "While this is entertaining, and I'm sure we would all like to hear of your exploits at some time in the future, I fail to see what this has to do with our current situation."

I nodded at him. "I know, but you didn't let me finish. Now, when the cops would catch me doing something I wasn't supposed to, they didn't try to arrest me. You know what they did?"

A rousing chorus of silence met this. *Tough crowd*, I thought.

"Well, I'll tell you what they did. Instead of jerking out their Tasers and handcuffs, they could make a call to the one person they knew could control me with *no effort at all.*"

Now I had their attention, by damn.

"Gentlemen, when the behemoth is raising hell, you don't call out the cops, you call…his *mother.*"

Odin began to grin. Pretty soon it was a full-fledged smile, and before you knew it, he was roaring laughter at the top of his voice. Heimdall joined after a few moments, but Thor, bless his little heart, just looked mystified. Heimdall looked over at him and, catching his breath from his laughter, said, "*Angrboda*, Thor! Loki is going to send Angrboda to get their son!"

Comprehension dawned on Thor's face and pretty soon he was laughing too. Trust me, seeing the Big Dogs of the Aesir laughing their guts out is a sight to behold. After a good long time, they finally calmed down enough to talk straight.

Odin said, "It makes perfect sense. Actually, Angrboda is the *only* person Loki could take Fenrir to, when you consider it. She would be the only creature in the Nine Worlds that could possibly exert any control over him, except Loki himself. So, Loki and Fenrir go to Angrboda, a nice family reunion, and they stay at her castle while she goes to fetch Jormungand. Then, they summon Hel and attack. I can't believe I didn't see this before." He slapped the table. "And to think, we were in Jotunheim that whole time, convinced Loki was elsewhere." The Allfather stood.

"Aesir and Einherjar, mount your steeds. We return to Jotunheim immediately."

Even with the loss of their brothers in that savage land earlier in the day, there was not a look of hesitation on a single face.

We were going back to Jotunheim, but this time, I was *not* carrying a single thing but myself. As a matter of fact, the damned horse was going to carry *me*. This, I could live with.

Chapter Nineteen

As we crossed over into Jotunheim, I asked Odin why we didn't just open a portal near Angrboda's castle and pull another surprise. His eye never left the trails, and we had scouts out in every direction, looking for any Giants that might be itching for a rematch. So far, it seemed like there weren't any. Odin spoke to me as he continued his vigilant survey of our route.

"We could have opened a portal there, Alexei. However, Utgard-Loki no doubt has all his sorcerers out in force, watching for just such an action. He cannot know how we defeated his enchantments, and will be looking for any magic that comes into being in his realm."

"But won't he be equally freaked out by a host of Aesir and Einherjar just riding through his kingdom?" I asked.

"Yes, no doubt he will be, which is exactly what I am counting on. I intend to make it seem as if we are marching straight to the Citadel again. By doing so, I

211

hope to force him into calling what is left of his armies to defend the Citadel against our attack. He cannot know our purpose. He may think we are simply coming back to gather the weapons of our fallen."

"But why wouldn't we just have taken them with us when we left, if that's what we're doing now?"

"Yes, that would have made much more sense, would it not? But I forget, you are not used to dealing with Giants. They are not the swiftest of thought, my son. Utgard-Loki is smarter than most, which is why he is king, but he is still only a Giant."

We pulled up as an Einherjar outrider came up with a report.

"The Giants are fleeing towards the Citadel, Allfather. Men, women, children, all of them. The way before us lies empty and deserted. There are sorcerers on some of the ridge tops, but for now, they do nothing but watch, and report back to Utgard-Loki, I am certain."

Odin nodded to the man, who turned his mount and galloped off in the direction from which he had come. Odin reached into a saddlebag and pulled out the map of Jotunheim I had seen earlier. Looking at it with him, I asked, "Where is Angrboda's castle?"

Odin looked around to see if we were being observed and said in a very quiet voice, "Do not speak so loudly, my son. It is said that even the rocks in Jotunheim have ears and report to its king."

I winced. So much for joining the Navy SEALS, I

thought. Odin pointed one gloved finger at a place marked by a simple dot. It was in a rugged area, with access by only a long narrow road that seemed to have deep chasms on either side. *Excellent*, I thought, *they can pick us off one at a time. That's just great.*

Seeing my distress, Odin clapped me on the shoulder. His voice still low, he said, "Worry not, my son. I have no intention of riding across that chasm. We will pass the entrance to her castle as if we intend to continue on to the Citadel. Once we have ridden past, I will open a portal and we will ride right up to her front door. Utgard-Loki will sense the magic at once, and I hope that causes even more of a panic than our company riding in plain view. Always try to throw your enemies into disarray at every opportunity, Alexei. Keep them guessing and off-guard."

It seemed I was learning a few things about warfare, after all. A sudden thought struck me. "Allfather, didn't the scout say that everyone was moving towards the Citadel? What if Angrboda is among those fleeing?"

"If Angrboda is indeed among those fleeing, then our plan has failed, my son, for she would never willingly leave her fastness if Loki and Fenrir are with her. She would not leave her lover or her son to face our army alone. She is proud, for a Giantess. Proud and evil. Evil without measure. Utgard-Loki himself has often proclaimed that it makes him nervous having her in his kingdom, for fear that she may one day decide that Jotunheim would fare better under a queen than a king." Odin laughed at this last. "Given today's events, he may well be right to fear that."

"How will we know if she is among the fleeing? I mean, will we know before we arrive at her castle and find out she's not home?"

Odin nodded. "We will know. I have placed three of my best scouts on the mountains that ring her castle. If she leaves, we will know."

"How long until we reach the road to her castle?" I asked, my voice still hushed.

Without turning his head, Odin said, "We are passing it now, on the left. Do not turn your head; look only with your eyes."

Damn, this was giving me a serious case of the willies. I mean, hadn't we just utterly defeated the armies of Jotunheim earlier today? This must be one bad-assed Giantess to warrant all this running around and covertness. Then again, this was the mother of three of the most horrible monsters in the Nine Worlds. I had a momentary image of the meanest Mama Bear in creation, and shook it away. From the corner of my eye, I could see the road, if you could call a narrow goat path that fell away into eternity on each side a road. I would have hated to have ridden over that if the Playmate of the Month was on the other end, let alone the horror we hoped was there.

We had traveled well beyond the turnoff to Angrboda's castle when another scout rode up from behind us. He gave me a nod, and then said to Odin, "Allfather, the Giantess is there. I saw her myself. She came out onto her highest turret to watch us pass, and then ran back inside."

Odin nodded again and thanked the scout. He rode off to fall in line with the rest of the company. I looked at Odin and asked, "Now what do we do? I mean, after you open the portal and we show up on her doorstep, that is. Do we knock, or demand her surrender, or what?"

Odin looked grimmer than I had ever seen him. His voice matched his expression. "Once we arrive in her courtyard, we must be prepared for the bloodiest battle that any of us has ever seen, I fear. Angrboda keeps a personal army of Giants loyal only to her, and known for their cruelty. The Einherjar can deal with them, I have no fear. However, while that is occurring, we must breach her castle, subdue Loki *and* Fenrir, as well as Angrboda herself, and then find a way to re-fetter the first two and restore balance to the Nine Worlds."

"Holy shit, how are supposed to do all *that*?!?"

He cast a glance my way. "Blasphemy, my son..."

I nearly choked, and then started laughing. "C'mon, Dad, cut me some slack. You lay all that on me and then jump me for 'holy shit'? I mean, that's not even aimed at any particular god."

"Still, the word 'holy' suggests religion... but I will let it go, just this once."

He said it deadpan, but I caught a glimmer of a smile around the corner of his mouth. Still laughing, I said, "So, really, how are we supposed to pull this off? Call me crazy, but I don't see Loki or Fenrir just throwing up their hands and saying 'All right, you got us, we quit.'"

The smile disappeared from Odin's face. "No, my son", he said heavily, "I do not see them doing that either."

"So what's the plan then?"

He looked at me for a long moment. Finally, he said, "Well, most of it depends on you, Alexei."

Now I choked in earnest. "Uh... Allfather... what, exactly, do you mean by that?"

His face was full of worry and sorrow, which went a long way to weakening my knees. I was glad I was on horseback, because I don't think I could have stood up on my own. "Alexei, you have a gift, a power, than none of us has ever heard of, much less seen. The Norns have been silent as to your role in all this, but I cannot think that your abilities are some fluke, some accident. At a time when we are closest to the end of all things, when our whole world has been completely upended after a thousand years, along comes the one man in all of the Nine Worlds that can do the things you do? I do not believe in coincidences, my son. You are here to see to it that all that has gone wrong is set aright, this I believe with all my soul."

Oh, shit. Well, there isn't any pressure here, right kids?

I looked into Odin's face to see if he was actually buying the crap he was saying, and I'll be damned if he didn't look just as honest as hell. His single eye shone out at me, and his entire bearing was relaxed and at ease. I'm no expert at reading body language, but judging from his stance, the Allfather truly believed that

I was somehow going to make everything all right.

Of course, if I fucked up, no big deal, only Ragnarok and the end of everything I have ever known and loved.

Sure, no sweat.

A sudden panic gripped me, so strong that I couldn't breathe, couldn't move. Odin's brow furrowed and he laid his hand on my shoulder. His voice sounded tinny, far away, but there was no mistaking the concern in it.

"Alexei? Son? What is it? Are you ill? Need I call for the healers?"

The vice that had wrapped itself around my body gave a little, and I was able to draw a short, painful breath. A few seconds later, I was able to draw another. My color must have alarmed Odin, because I could hear him calling for Heimdall in that tinny, far-away voice.

Heimdall reached my side and wonder of wonders; he seemed to know exactly what was wrong. As the Allfather looked on worriedly, Heimdall spoke gently and quietly into my right ear. His voice was soothing, although it took me several seconds to make out what he was saying.

"Breathe, little brother, just breathe. In and out. Slowly, now. All is well, we are here with you, and we are going nowhere. Breathe."

Odin leaned in close to me to look into my face, his face a mask of concern and worry. "What ails him, Heimdall? Is it an enchantment of some kind? If so, we have lost all surprise."

Heimdall glanced at me, and then looked at the Allfather. "What were you talking about before Alexei became so affected?"

As Odin related our conversation, Heimdall began shaking his head. By the time the Allfather was finished, Heimdall actually looked angry. His voice held a definite edge when he spoke. "What in the name of the Nine Worlds were you thinking, Father? You have nearly frightened Alexei into a state of pure panic."

Odin looked affronted. The edge in his voice more than met the one in Heimdall's. "And since when is it a bad thing to express one's trust and confidence in one's brothers in arms?" His eye glinted dangerously.

Heimdall blew out a deep breath and calmed down. When he answered the Allfather, his voice was much more respectful. "Father, we continually hold Alexei to our standards and expectations. We forget that he is mortal, a human. What is commonplace to us is something quite different to him."

Odin looked confused. "But I was merely telling him that he will succeed in the upcoming battle, and that through his actions, Ragnarok will be avoided…" Odin's voice trailed away, and a look of understanding crossed his face. Shaking his head, he turned to me and said, "Once again, it seems I must beg your forgiveness, my son. I never even thought of how you must be feeling, the pressure you are under. I am very sorry." His voice was contrite, and I couldn't help but smile at him in the hopes of removing that awful look of shame from his face. Finally finding enough breath to form words, I said to him, "It's okay, Allfather. It's just a very large chunk to have to swallow. I think I was going under the assumption that we had a plan here."

Now Odin *did* give me a smile. A wide, face-changing smile that caused his remaining eye to crinkle into nonexistence. With a laugh, he said, "But of course we have a plan, my son! I am astounded that you would think that we would not!"

A huge weight fell from my shoulders, and the band around my chest loosened immensely. With a weak grin, I managed, "Thanks for that. I was kinda worried for a minute there. So, what's the plan?"

Although I would have said it was impossible, Odin's grin stretched even further across his face. If it kept going, his lips would meet at the back of his neck, and the top of his head would fall off. With a roar of absolute delight, he said, "The plan, my gifted son, is simplicity itself: We enter the portal, and come out in Angrboda's courtyard. And then we kill everything we see. Easy enough, yes?"

Although the bands snapped back around my chest, they weren't as tight as before. As I sat watching the Allfather of the Aesir laugh like a complete lunatic, I was shocked to find myself joining him. The laughter found its way from the bottom of my feet and surged throughout my body like a great healing fire. I was dimly aware of Heimdall laughing at my side. *What a sight we must make*, I thought.

Once our laughter had tapered off into the occasional hiccup, we stood facing each other. Thor and Tyr had rode up during our outburst, but seemed to find nothing at all odd about the three of us howling like monkeys. They had simply stood with slight grins on their faces. Now, the five of us faced each other, and all around us, the thousands of Einherjar. A quiet calm descended over us, even the wind seemed to hold its breath in anticipation. Odin looked about and raised his voice like thunder.

"My Einherjar, you have proven yourselves a thousand times over, both before the Valkyries came for you and since. There is not a man among you that I do not feel honored to stand beside in battle, or drink beside at my table." This evoked a laughing cheer from the mass of men. As impossible as it must have been, Odin seemed to look each man in the eye. "We go now to right a wrong, and return to the Nine Worlds the balance and peace they deserve. Is this not our calling? Is this not our purpose? Are we not the wall of justice and honor that all evil and vile things must break against? Are you not my NORSEMEN???"

The roar of the Einherjar was so great that the sound of it must have carried throughout all the Nine Worlds. With my newfound resolve, I found myself hoping that it reached Loki, Fenrir, and Angrboda, at least. Let them know that we were here, we were coming, and we were *pissed*.

Odin turned in a full circle, his gaze taking in his massive army. "Now, my Einherjar, my brothers, let us RIDE ON TO GLORY!!!!" He flung his hand, and a portal far larger than any I had seen before ripped open the very air in front of us. Raising Gungnir, he spurred his horse into a full gallop into the portal.

He did not ride alone.

Row after row, thousands upon thousands, the Aesir and the Einherjar charged into the portal, the bloodlust of battle surging in their veins.

I found myself very glad I rode *with* these men, and was not one of those that waited on the other side.

Chapter Twenty

From within the dank stone walls of Angrboda's castle, Loki watched through an arrow slit as the hated Aesir rode past with their wretched Einherjar. His two-tone eyes glittered with a hatred so great that it seemed that they were sure to erupt from his head at the slightest provocation. Unable to stand still, he paced from one arrow slit to the next, constantly moving. Oddly enough, Fenrir was laying calmly in the center of the tower, his mother stroking his lank fur.

Angrboda was sitting in her massive chair, its arms and legs made from the bones of her enemies, its leather made from their skin. At the moment, she wore a beatific smile, which on her was more horrible than any scowl. She was not unattractive, as far as Giants go, and in her youth had been quite lovely. That youth was long gone now, and years uncounted of hate had contorted her face into permanent positions, positions that were not flattering. From the corner of his eyes, Loki looked at her, wondering what it was about her he had found so attractive in years gone by. She was nothing compared to the beauty of Sigyn, of that there could be no doubt. Sigyn looked a million times better just awakening than Angrboda could if she put in a weeks' worth of primping.

What was it, wondered Loki. What was it about this Giantess that had so captured his lust? For lust was all it ever had been, he knew that. The creature had spawned three of his children, each more horrible than the previous. Sigyn had been faithful, beautiful, and loving. Angrboda was the negative image of all of these traits.

A spark of sanity shot through the whirlwind of madness that made up his usual thoughts and Loki found himself wondering what he was doing here with this horrid creature and the reeking spawn she had foisted upon him. He was a blood-brother of Odin, for the love of all. He had once been a welcome member of the Aesir, standing by their sides in times of peace and war. Of course he had sometimes taken his little jokes too far, but had he not made amends each time he had overstepped himself?

He found himself thinking again of Sigyn, and wondered where she was. Suddenly, it snapped in his mind, the events of these last days. Sigyn was dead, and by his own hand. How had he killed her? He was genuinely lost for a moment. A knife or some such? That wasn't quite right. He began obsessively trying to remember what had happened to his wife. He began pacing again, mumbling under his breath.

"No, not a knife. An axe? No, damn it all, not an axe either. What was it? What was it…?"

From her chair, Angrboda stopped stroking Fenrir for a moment. The huge wolf whined like a puppy. She stared at Loki for a long moment. He was not himself. Of course, with Loki, being himself was never the same from one moment to the next. Angrboda was used to this, but his actions since he had arrived at her door with her beloved son were off-kilter, even for *him*.

"What bothers you so, Loki my love? Why do you pace? The forever-damned Aesir ride to the Citadel to gloat over their victory this day, and soon we will have all our children here with us. Once we all stand together, no force in the Nine Worlds will be able to withstand us. Is this not pleasing to you, my love?"

Loki stared at her blankly, his eyes twirling wildly. After a moment, he said, "Was it a mace? I don't own a mace. So no, it could not have been a mace. It was shiny, this I remember..." With this, he resumed his pacing and muttering.

Angrboda began to feel serious reservations about this family reunion. She had already sent a message to Hel, telling her to stand ready to join in the destruction when the time came. It was nearing time for Angrboda to slip into Midgard and fetch Jormungand. She needed only the Aesir to be far enough past her mountain fastness so as not to notice the ripple in the fabric of the worlds when she passed through. They would be far enough away soon, but Angrboda now didn't know exactly how she felt leaving Loki here alone with Fenrir. The man was clearly not balanced, and he could upset things greatly if he decided to attack the Aesir with her army before she returned with the Midgard Serpent. She had no intention of going through all the trouble of dragging her massive son into this world, only to find her army slaughtered, her castle destroyed. In a quiet voice, she tried again to bring Loki around.

"Loki, my love, we need to prepare. Jormungand will be here soon, as will Hel. Once our children are gathered, we must be ready to attack. I will sit on the throne of Jotunheim ere this night ends, and you will sit upon Odin's throne. Will that not be the greatest trophy of all?"

Loki stopped dead in front of her. "What did you say?" he asked, his eyes twirling wildly. "What did you just say to me?"

Angrboda actually found herself recoiling from his gaze. Finding her courage she repeated, "That I will sit, Queen of Jotunheim, and you will sit on the throne of the defeated Allfather, this will be the greatest trophy of all."

Loki gave out an enormous yell and began to dance in place. Angrboda and Fenrir exchanged confused and frightened looks. Loki danced and leapt around the room, sometimes kicking heels together like a minstrel. He clapped his hands and began to sing in a horrid, atonal voice, "Trophy, trophy, it was a damned trophy! Trophy, trophy, a damned trophy from MEEEEE!!!!"

Angrboda and Fenrir were now both on their feet and as far away from Loki as they could get in the circular room. Fenrir growled, a rumble that could be felt throughout the floor, and Angrboda had her hands up in a defensive position, prepared to strike.

Loki capered for a moment or two more, and then suddenly stopped. He glanced around at his companion and his son, his face a mask of utter calm. When he spoke, the madness that had so heavily laden his voice a moment before was gone. A cold and logical tone replaced it. "It was a trophy I killed her with. A bowling trophy, if memory serves." He flapped his hand dismissively at them. "Neither of you were with me at the time, so it doesn't matter."

Angrboda and Fenrir gave each other another uneasy look. Before either could ask Loki what he was talking about, he spun on his heel and clapped his hands together. "So!" he said forcefully, "What next? I assume you are prepared to bring Jormungand here, Angrboda? And that Hel has been informed of our plans?"

Relieved that Loki's brief storm of madness had passed, Angrboda nodded eagerly. "I am simply waiting until the Aesir have passed beyond my lands to fetch our other son. I do not wish to give them any time to prepare, and they might sense me passing through the worlds if they are too near. They will soon be nearing the Citadel, and I can bring Jormungand here, and Hel will soon follow." She looked to Loki for his endorsement of her plan.

Loki was staring out the arrow slit once again, tapping his foot in time to music only he could seem to hear. When he spoke, his voice was unconcerned and light, as if they were planning a tea party rather than the end of the world. "So, you wish to wait until the Aesir are past your lands before you go after Jormungand?"

"Yes", said Angrboda, nodding eagerly. "Once they are far enough away, victory will be ours completely."

Loki nodded pleasantly. His voice still light, he said,

"Well, I sincerely hope that you have some sort of back-up plan to all of this."

Angrboda began to grow irritated. "No, my love, I do *not* have a 'back-up' plan, as you put it. I think the plan I have will work just fine. Unless, of course, the mighty *Loki* has a better one?"

Loki, still smiling, said, "Nope, I don't. As a matter of fact, I didn't have a main plan, let alone a back-up. I just sort of... you know... roll with things. I figured once I had freed Fenrir and gotten Utgard-Loki on board, everything else would just sort of fall into place." He continued to look out of the arrow slit. "Unfortunate that you don't have a back-up plan, though, because your first one is fucked."

Angrboda shot past irritated and into furious. "Well, *mighty* Loki, my love, why don't you point out all my glaring errors, so I may learn from your vast wisdom?"

Loki whipped away from the arrow slit and headed towards the stairwell. As he past Angrboda, he said calmly, "Well, the most glaring error I can see is that the Aesir and Einherjar are currently filling up your courtyard, and there isn't a single Giant out there to welcome them properly. Beyond that, I'm sure I'll find a few other things wrong along the way."

Angrboda rushed to the arrow slit and was horrified to see Loki had been speaking the truth. From a huge shimmering portal, Aesir and Einherjar were pouring into her courtyard; too many to even begin to count. Through the haze of the portal, she could see the ranks still coming stretching as far as she could see.

She gave out a scream of frustration, and turned to follow Loki down the stairwell, Fenrir at her heels.

As she came up behind Loki, he stopped and looked over his shoulder and said casually, "Don't ever call me 'my love' again, you huge bitch. I mean *really*. Haven't you ever heard the term 'booty call'? Jeez." With that, he began running down the stairs.

Angrboda and Fenrir could only stand, mouths (or jaws) agape.

Chapter Twenty-One

As we charged through the portal, I drew my sword. I don't know exactly what it was I was expecting once I gained the far side of the portal, but an empty stone courtyard wasn't it. Apparently, that was a feeling shared by the rest of my companions, as well. We looked at each other in confusion, but pressed on, simply because the rest of the Einherjar were right behind us and charging hell-for-leather through the portal. Odin gave a signal, and the bulk of our warriors began to fan out, making concentric circles around the courtyard. This helped a little, but we were still far too bunched up, and were beginning to trample one another.

Close to Odin, I yelled over the din, "Allfather, have you ever heard of a place called Thermopylae?" I could tell by the look of concern in his eye that he had. Thor, overhearing me, yelled, "I just watched the movie '300' the other day! A fine film! What was the name of the actor that played Leonidas?"

I could tell we were about to get into a drawn-out

discussion about the many attributes of Gerard Butler when Odin cut us off. I mentally sent a "thank you" his way. To Thor, he yelled, "We are getting hemmed in here, Thor! We make fine targets, all in a bunch like this. Do you think you might do something to remedy that?"

Thor looked confused, surprise, surprise. Odin looked to the sky and closed his single eye. Taking a steadying breath, he looked back at Thor, mimed swinging a hammer, and pointed at the high stone walls that enclosed us.

Thor remained stupefied. Shaking my head, I brought my mount close to his and yelled, "Use Mjollnir to smash down the walls, you big dork! Give us some room to maneuver!"

A look of comprehension crossed his face, and he pulled his massive hammer from his belt. He prepared to strike, and then glanced at me with suspicion. "What is a dork?" he demanded.

Laughing like a lunatic, I told him I would tell him later. He gave me another suspicious glance and then a curt nod. He said, "You may want to move back a bit", and began swinging his hammer in circles over his head. I was all for moving out of the way, but I was pretty much trapped where I was, seeing as the Einherjar hadn't stopped pouring through the portal. I had to make do with ducking low on my horse and trying to breathe, as each swing sucked the air out of my lungs.

With a roar, Thor launched Mjollnir at the wall. I expected a pretty big hole, but as the dust settled, I was amazed to see the wall had simply exploded into dust for as far as I could see in both directions. Nodding at Thor, I said, "Way to go, big brother." He nodded back and said, "Remember it when you are explaining to me what a 'dork' is." I didn't have a come-back for that.

Seeing the wall gone, Odin began giving orders for the Einherjar to encircle the castle and destroy any resistance they encountered. These were orders that the Einherjar could totally get behind. In an amazingly short amount of time, the courtyard held only the Aesir and a few hundred Einherjar that had elected to remain close to the Allfather. Thor had attempted to charge through the rest of the men, but Odin called him back. Once he was back with us, grumbling under his breath, Odin began speaking.

"This is *not* what I had expected. Either they are not here, or we have so surprised them that they were unable to mount a defense."

At that moment, the sound of battle began to be heard all around the castle. Instinctively, Thor and Tyr moved towards it, but Odin summoned them back. He looked over at Heimdall. The Aesir nodded and closed his eyes for a moment. When he opened them, they were full of gold light. I caught my breath. This was not something I had seen Heimdall do before, and I wasn't sure what was happening. After a few seconds, Heimdall spoke.

"The Giants loyal to Angrboda are attempting to defend the castle. However, they were given no orders to do so by the Giantess, and as such, were totally unprepared. They are being defeated quite handily all around us. We seemed to have surprised them utterly."

With that, Heimdall closed his eyes for a second. When they reopened, they were their normal sky-blue.

"What the hell was *that*, big brother?" I asked. "You know any other cool party tricks *I* should know about?"

He laughed. "I am the Watchman of the Aesir, Alexei, remember? I can see everything, hear everything, and I never sleep."

I nodded. "That not sleeping thing must really suck, bro."

He sighed. "You have no idea." He suddenly looked tired and forlorn, but snapped out of it as Odin began speaking.

"Well, it seems that our surprise certainly worked, but as I do not see Jormungand, I can only hope we are not too late to catch our quarry."

"I'm terribly sorry that Jormungand isn't here at the moment", came a voice that sent a shudder down my spine. Imagine the most horrid thing you can, multiply it by a million, and then give it a voice. That's about what we're dealing with here.

We all turned to see Loki leaning in the massive doorway of the castle, his arms crossed nonchalantly across his chest. I could sense the Aesir tense around me, and I thought that it might not be a bad idea to tense right along with them. Loki continued, his voice ringing out far too clearly for my liking.

"You see, my son was *supposed* to be here, but due to some bad timing, he had not arrived when you did.

Well, one of my sons, anyway. Fenrir is here, aren't you, my boy?"

There was an enormous growl from behind Loki and Fenrir sprang over his head and landed with a thud between his father and the Aesir. If I hadn't been standing in the presence of the Allfather, Heimdall, Thor, and Tyr, I might have turned tail and ran like hell. To tell the truth, if I hadn't been hemmed in by the Einherjar, I may have done it anyway. What was standing in the courtyard wasn't a wolf by any definition I could come up with, but I guess that's as close as it comes. It was furry and had teeth, anyway.

Oh, and by the way, it was fucking *terrifying*.

Fenrir opened his massive jaws (giving me a far better look at his teeth than I needed) and said, "Tyr... my old playmate. How good of you to come. I have missed our time together. Tell me, have the Aesir ever thanked you for sacrificing your hand to tether me? Or have they even mentioned it at all?"

Tyr sat on his horse, his face carved of stone. In a flat voice, he said, "I would have gladly sacrificed my neck if that had been what it would have taken to tether you, Fenrir. Once, you were my friend. You became something else. Now, you are nothing to me at all except an enemy to be killed."

Fenrir roared and flung his head from side to side, the saliva from his massive teeth nearly reaching where we stood, almost fifty yards away. The foamy globs fell with loud *splats* onto the stone courtyard. When he had regained his temper, Fenrir looked at Tyr with an utter loathing. "You will find it a shade more difficult to kill me than you suspect, Tyr." The wolf allowed his gaze to travel over the rest of the assemblage. "I suspect all of you together cannot kill me, as a matter of fact. I will enjoy eating each of you, one…at…a…time." Fenrir tensed to spring, and we all gripped our weapons tighter in anticipation when Loki spoke again. This time, his voice was pleasant and happy. I was amazed at the change. *What the fuck,* I thought in shock, *this guy could sell gasoline to a guy on fire!*

"Come now, my son, is that any way to treat our guests? Uninvited though they may be, we are still their hosts, and is it not our way to treat guests with respect and honor?" Fenrir relaxed, looking confused, and gave a little whine. Loki moved from his spot by the door and strolled towards us as if we were all long-time friends, just dropping by for a bit of lunch and some catching up. When he had gotten to within a few feet of Odin, the Allfather lowered Gungnir until the tip was pointed at Loki's throat. Amazingly, Loki never stopped until the tip of the spear rested firmly against his flesh. With a dazzling smile, he looked up at Odin and shook his finger at him.

"Now, now, Odin. Is that any way to treat an old friend and sworn blood-brother?" He spread his hands, showing that he was weaponless. "I would have expected better from the Allfather of the Aesir, at least as far as manners go. The rest of this bunch…" He let his voice trail off as he cast his eyes over us. When they reached me, I couldn't help but give a twitch. Trust me; having the two-toned eyes of a complete psychopath trained on you is a bit disconcerting. Loki, however, positively radiated good cheer and happiness at having seen me. Without so much as a backward glance at Odin, he turned and walked over to my horse. Even having the advantage of looking down at him, I felt very out of my depth.

"You simply *must* be Alexei Addison", he said. I nodded. "Oh, my, how glad I am to finally meet you! You have no idea how much I have waited for this moment!"

I remembered Isaac Macintyre, the poor kid down the hall from my dorm room and amazed myself by saying, "Yeah, I have a pretty good idea of how much you wanted to meet me, you crazy-eyed fuck. Believe me, the feeling goes both ways. I'm gonna enjoy rearranging what's left of your face, asshole."

Thor and Heimdall looked at each other and then roared laughter. Even dour Tyr cracked a grin. Only Odin remained expressionless.

For a split-second, the façade of Loki's charm slipped, and I got a glimpse of the murderous hatred that lay just beneath it. *Dammit*, I said to myself, *I am going to have a surgery to have my mouth permanently welded shut.* In a blink of an eye, Loki was just as pleasant as before. "Well", he said, "We'll just have to see about that, now won't we?" Marking me with one more lingering glance, he returned to Odin.

"State your purpose, Allfather. You've brought illegal warfare to Jotunheim twice this day. Have the Norns gone on vacation, or are all the rules that bind the Nine Worlds no longer in effect?"

Odin's voice made ice seem balmy. "The Norns are where they always are, Loki, but the rules that bind the Nine Worlds *have* been bent, if not broken. Do not test my patience playing your games. You and yours are the reasons those rules find themselves under such strain."

Loki looked shocked. "You mean it's *my* fault things aren't going according to plan in the universe? Oh, then for the sake of the cosmos, let's get me re-fettered to that rock so that serpent can drip poison on my face forever, shall we? Of course, Fenrir will have to be re-fettered, as well, but I'm sure he won't mind, will you, son?" This elicited a terrible growl from Fenrir. Loki paid no mind, but continued, "Of course, I don't know what we'll use to fetter either of us now. You see, those helpful humans destroyed my son's intestines when the freed me, and Fenrir has seen through the lies that held him in place." Loki snapped his fingers, as if just remembering something. "Oh, and another thing, I suppose I will just have to suffer the venom of the serpent constantly without Sigyn there to catch some of it in her precious little bowl. But no matter. Quickly, let's set everything right in the Nine Worlds. After all I just want to do my part." The sarcasm in his voice was now so thick you could have cut it.

"You're right about Sigyn", I said. "I doubt she'll be in the mood to give you a hand anymore. I think you can consider yourself divorced at this point."

Loki whipped his head around like a striking snake. "Yes, little *human*, I suppose I can, seeing as she is dead, although I would think that would make me more of a widower, don't you?"

I smiled. "Sigyn isn't dead, you circus freak. She was just fine when I left her bed in Fensalir. She is staying with Frigg until we get this shit straightened out." The fact that nothing sexual had occurred in that bed was well-known by everyone here except Loki and Fenrir, and I saw no reason to give him the satisfaction.

I finally managed to get under Loki's skin, and in a big way. His already horribly scarred face seemed to writhe as if there were living things under the skin. His eyes twirled so fast that it was like looking at a painted top freshly spun. All the pleasantry and happiness that had filled his voice was gone now, evaporated like dew in the sun. He couldn't speak at first; only make incoherent noises at me. Finally, he was able to vent his rage.

"You lying son of a human whore! My wife is dead! I know, for it was *I THAT KILLED HER*!!! Your lies are as pathetic as your false courage, *mortal*!"

I sat calmly on my horse, and arranged my face into what I hoped was disgusted contempt. "Yes, we know all about how the brave and fearless Loki killed the most beautiful and loyal creature to have ever been a part of his life. Killed her with *a bowling trophy*, no less, how incredibly original you are! The stories that will be told of your mighty conquests… wait… you don't really have any, do you? All you've got is a fucked up face, stupid-looking eyes, and a treasure trove of disgusting kids. No, Loki, I don't think you'll make the grade when it comes time to tell the tales of the Aesir."

I thought I had finally managed to push him too far. I don't know what I expected to happen. I was playing it by ear, just like I had been since Heimdall had shown up outside my dorm room. So far, that had worked for me the best.

Loki stood trembling, his fists clenching and unclenching in rage. My companions said nothing, but merely sat looking expectantly at Loki. I guessed they had decided to follow my lead. If I wanted to goad Loki into single combat, I suppose that was within their odd, yet honorable set of rules. For a second, I thought I was going to find out for sure, but then Loki stopped trembling and took a deep breath. Without giving me so much as a glance, he looked into Odin's eye. "Is what the human says true, Allfather? On our blood-oath, does Sigyn live?"

Odin seemed taken aback by the question, but nodded soberly. "It is *because* of the human that she lives, Loki. She was giving herself up to the mists when he stopped her." Loki looked surprised by that, but said nothing. After a moment, he turned to me again. His voice was now neither charming nor frightening. It was simply a normal voice, perhaps his true one.

"I owe you a debt, human, although I am loathe to say it. I regret my actions in regard to Sigyn, and I am glad she is well." His face darkened. "Do not think that this means I will not wear your skin as a coat, mortal, because I will. This merely means I will have to wear it with humility instead of gloating about it."

"Gee, thanks", I mumbled.

Odin had finally seemed to have had enough of a reunion to suit him. "Loki, you have committed atrocities in Midgard, and have tried to bring about

Ragnarok before its fated time. For these actions, you will be re-fettered, as will Fenrir. Your torment will last until it is truly time for Ragnarok to commence. At that time, you may do as you will, as the Norns will allow. I await that day with great impatience, for I long to see you dead and gone from this universe."

Well, I thought, *that is just about the name of that tune.*

Apparently, I was wrong again. From behind us rode up one of the Einherjar. He was covered in dirt, sweat, and blood, but he was grinning from ear to ear. To Odin, he said, "Allfather, the army of Angrboda is slain. They asked for no quarter, so none was given." Odin nodded, as if he had expected this.

Angrboda, however, had not.

With a scream that made me fear my ears were bleeding, the Giantess came slamming out of her castle. She was certainly large. Large and incredibly pissed off. Oh, and very, very armed to the teeth. She made a beeline for Odin, marking him for the author of all her misery. Loki just stood watching, as if something interesting had just come on T.V. Angrboda prepared to throw her axe (one of many she was wearing on her person), when I saw a flicker of movement from Odin. Faster than I could follow, he flung Gungnir towards Angrboda. The Giantess took two more steps, but the axe in her hand fell to the earth behind her. She opened her mouth to speak, but an enormous glut of blood issued forth instead. With a look of shock, she glanced down at her chest. Gungnir was sticking halfway through her, and blood poured down her chest. She raised her eyes toward Loki in desperation, but he merely shrugged his shoulders as if to say *and what did you expect?* With a strange gracefulness, the Giantess slid to her knees. She looked once more at Loki, and her eyes lost their focus. She fell backwards, but only made it halfway. Gungnir stuck into the ground behind her, and she hung like that, arms falling behind her, looking towards the sky.

At least until she started sliding down the shaft of the spear, and then I found something else to look at.

Fenrir had been relatively quiet up to this point, but at seeing his mother killed in front of him, he went mad. Or madder, I guess I should say. With a howl of such fury and pain that it nearly cut into me, the wolf charged us, crazed beyond reason. I saw Loki open his mouth to say something, and then change his mind. He instead moved gracefully out of the line of fire and watched to see what would happen next.

Fenrir covered the fifty yards in a single bound. I dimly heard Odin yell that they *mustn't* kill Fenrir, they *mustn't!*

Then it hit me like a ton of bricks. I closed my eyes. Loki, the Trickster, had known it all along. Both he and Fenrir were instrumental to the coming of Ragnarok. Without their participation, that battle could not come to its set conclusion. While that seemed like a great thing in a way, I realized that fucking with the Norns, the Fates, whatever you wanted to call it, just couldn't be done. Loki and Fenrir had to be front and center at Ragnarok, because the humans that had brought them into existence had said so. Change that, and you unravel the whole of the universe. If Loki or Fenrir died today, Ragnarok happened *now.* Incredibly, I smelled my mother's chocolate chip cookies, and thought of my parents, sitting in our little house in Kentucky. Without any conscious thought, I screamed "STOP!" at the top of my voice.

I opened my eyes to see that Fenrir had, indeed, stopped. As a matter of fact, he hung in the air just a few feet from the massed weapons of my companions. That blue light I had been given was covering the wolf, pulsating in time with my heartbeat. Fenrir's eyes rolled around wildly, but he could not move a muscle. Okay, one problem dealt with.

Odin brought my attention to the other problem just as it was about to slide a dagger into my throat. Loki had a look of determination on his face that gave me the willies, just seeing it. Again, I acted without conscious thought, and suddenly Loki found himself in the same shape as his son. I blew out a breath as I noticed just how close the dagger was to my throat. A half a second more, and I would have been minus a windpipe and most of my blood. My horse skittered backwards and I nearly lost my concentration on Loki and Fenrir. This could get bad quickly. To Odin, I yelled, "Allfather, open a portal to Lyngvi!"

Odin looked confused. "Why do you wish to go to Lyngvi, my son?"

I didn't have time to be properly respectful. Well, Thor could just kick my ass later, I supposed. "Odin! Lyngvi! NOW!!!"

This seemed to suit the Allfather, although I could see Thor's face harden. Man, talk about dense.

Odin swept his hand, and a portal, much smaller

than the one that had brought us here, opened before us. I began to ride towards it, seeing the darkness of Lyngvi through the haze. Loki and Fenrir followed behind me like a couple of incredibly fucked-up Thanksgiving Day floats. I heard Odin yelling orders to the Einherjar, and then I passed through the portal.

Going from the cold, windswept hills of Jotunheim to the dark, clammy island of Lyngvi was almost enough for me to lose my concentration. Loki seemed to sense that, and struggled as hard as he could against my field. The same could be said for Fenrir, now that he saw his old prison again. I concentrated, and the blue light glowed brighter. Once I had them completely immobile again, I looked around.

Not that there was much to see, but I figured that the boulder that had held Fenrir for so long was just what the doctor ordered. Even busted in half, it would serve. Focusing my mind, I sent both of them slamming into the boulder, probably a little harder than was necessary, but what the hell, I'd had a pretty tough day.

A hand fell on my shoulder and I turned to see Odin beside me. Thor was off to one side, speaking with Tyr. Heimdall walked up to me on my other side and for a few moments I just stood between them, enjoying the strength they had to give me. Looking at my captives, I focused my energy again and suddenly Loki and Fenrir were bound to the boulder by bands of glowing blue light instead of being entirely encapsulated. This was easier for me to do, and it seemed to work fine. The downside was that they could now both speak and were doing so, at full volume. With a snarl of my own, two more blue bands appeared, these two across the mouths of my captives.

Odin clapped my shoulder and said, "That was quick thinking, my son. I must admit I was unsure how to proceed back there. Had we killed them, or had they killed us…"

He didn't have to finish that train of thought.

"Well, we've got them here for now, at least", I said. "That should give us some breathing room. What next, though? I mean, I'm tapped in the ideas department."

Odin and Heimdall shared a look. I could tell that they were just as tapped as I was. God, I was tired. I sat down on the ground and leaned back on my elbows. Looking up at the darkness above me, I could feel myself drifting off. Well, the hell with it. Let *them* figure something out. I'd done my good deed for the day.

I wasn't even sure what had happened until I felt the blood running from my mouth. One second, I'm drifting off, and the next it felt like the side of my face had caved in. I saw stars and had a ringing in my left ear. Reaching up to wipe the blood from my mouth I looked up at Heimdall. Trying to keep the rage out of my voice, I said, "Is that some sort of Norse 'thank you' ritual, or did you just decide you wanted to slap the shit out of someone?"

Heimdall had the decency to look ashamed, but when he pointed at the boulder and its occupants, I caught on to the reason for the slap. While I had been starting to doze off, the blue light had begun to fade from Loki and Fenrir. A few seconds more, and they would have been completely free. It didn't take a rocket scientist to figure out who they would have attacked first, either, since both of them were shooting murderous glances my way.

"Well, thanks for the heads-up, Heimdall, but a simple 'Hey Alexei' would have sufficed."

Again, he looked abashed. "Perhaps, little brother, but I acted on impulse. I apologize for striking you so hard. Are you all right?"

"Yeah, I'm fine. Just feels like I got kicked in the face by a bull, that's all."

Loki was laughing his scarred head off. I hadn't gotten his muzzle back on yet. I was about to fix that when he stopped laughing. He looked at me quizzically. Before I shut him up, he asked me in a quiet voice, "How long can you stay awake, mortal? And even should you be able to maintain wakefulness forever, are you prepared to remain here that long? I'm sure we could have long conversations about what my son and I will do to your corpse once you die of old age."

I was about to hit him with a snappy come-back when I realized that the son of a bitch was one hundred percent correct. What was I going to do now? I turned and looked at Odin and Heimdall, the look of fear obvious on my face. They reached out in unison and took me by the arms, leading me away from Loki.

"Allfather, Loki's right", I said. "I can't stay awake forever. The second I fall asleep, they'll be free. I mean, I'll stay awake as long as I can, but…" I stopped, at a loss for words. Finally, I said, "Is there no magic, no spell that can keep me awake, like Heimdall?"

Odin nodded, but looked troubled. "There are such enchantments, but what about…"

"What?" I asked.

He hesitated. "You are mortal, my son. You will not live forever. When you die, your power will dissipate, and we will be right back where we are now."

I thought for a second, and dredged up a memory from that long-ago report on the Vikings. "How about Idun's apples?" I could see Odin and Heimdall both jerk in surprise. "Well, I mean, if I eat her apples, won't I stay young forever, like you?"

I could see Odin thinking, his brows knitting together. Finally, he said, "Yes, my son, you would remain as you are now. And with the enchantments, you would never sleep. But, my son…Alexei… do you truly understand what it is you are saying?"

I opened my mouth to say sure, and then it hit me like a wave. I would be young forever. I would never sleep again. And most importantly, I would spend eternity in this dark, stinking cavern, with only Loki and Fenrir for company. I would never see my parents again, or even my own world. I would merely be a place-keeper, a guardian until Ragnarok actually came around. I looked over at Heimdall as I mulled this over. Suddenly, his role in the cosmos seemed one whole hell of a lot tougher than I had originally thought. Seeing me looking at me, he gave me a sad smile. Yes, of all the Aesir, he alone could truly know what I was about to undertake.

After a long time, I finally looked at Odin. With a

sigh, I said, "Yes, Allfather, I understand." A thought of my mother shot through my mind, her dimpled smile when she saw me coming through the door. My jaw set and I said again, "Yes, I understand completely. I am prepared to do this."

To my utter amazement, Odin's eye misted over, and a single tear ran down his bearded face. He reached out towards me, and I expected the customary clap on the shoulder. Instead, I found myself engulfed in a hug so fierce I lost my breath. When he pulled back, I was leaking about the eyes a little myself. Looking at Heimdall, I saw that he was crying openly, without shame. Thor seemed to find the far side of the island interesting, but I could have sworn I heard a sniffle. Tyr looked at me, his eyes dry, but he did the next best thing: without ever taking his eyes off mine, he placed his hand over his heart and then spread his fingers out to me. I nodded back, aware of the honor that he had given me.

Odin now held me at arm's length, his strong hands gripping my shoulders. His voice quivered with emotion when he spoke.

"Alexei Addison, you are my son of mortal blood. When Heimdall brought you before me, I knew not what sort of man you were. I had hopes, but I knew nothing of your heart. I say this now, in the presence of these Aesir: Never have I been prouder than I am now. That you would sacrifice your life is one thing. All men owe the Norns a death. But you would sacrifice something so much more. You would sacrifice your life, your death, your *eternity*, so that all in the Nine Worlds can go about their lives. And you would do so knowing that there would be so very few that even know of this sacrifice." He stopped a moment. I thought he was getting himself back under the iron control that I had seen him exert over himself since I had met him. At last, he spoke again.

"You may think you are good enough to make this sacrifice, Alexei, but I do not." Seeing my hurt confusion, he went quickly on. "I think you are *too* good for this sacrifice. You are far too good a man to be wasted in this dismal place, in the company of these… creatures."

He turned to Heimdall. "Go and tell the Norns where we now stand, and tell them that Odin, Allfather of the Aesir, demands their audience… *now.*"

From the collected gasps, I could tell that this wasn't a common occurrence. Clearing his throat, Heimdall said, "Allfather… is that demand… *wise?* The Norns are not used to obeying orders. *Anyone's* orders."

Odin's single eye blazed, and Heimdall took an involuntary step back. "I'm certain that they are not used to obeying orders, and I'm *equally* sure that they are going to point that out when you give them mine. When they do, ask them if they are used to having to have the entire fate of the Nine Worlds restored to balance by a mortal from Midgard. If they refuse to come, tell them that I am fully prepared to release Loki and Fenrir, and Ragnarok's timetable be damned."

Again came the collective gasp. From what I could gather, the Allfather was royally pissed, and was going to get his way. His threat about releasing Loki and

Fenrir was just that, a threat.

I hoped.

Chapter Twenty-Two

Heimdall was gone just long enough for me to get anxious and Odin to get even more pissed. Finally, after what seemed and eternity, a portal opened and through it stepped a rather pale Heimdall, followed by three identical women, except one was a blonde, one was a brunette, and one was a redhead. Beyond that, I could in no way tell them apart. They were strikingly beautiful, and seemed to be in their mid-thirties, but who the hell can tell with immortals?

They stepped regally up to Odin, and each had a small moue of distaste evident on their mouths. It was obvious that they weren't used to being beckoned anywhere, and sure as hell not someplace as unpleasant as *this*. The redhead stepped up to Odin and said, "So, what is so important that the Allfather now thinks he can summon the Norns when he feels the need?"

Sarcasm, anyone?

Ignoring this, Odin turned to me and raised his hands towards the women. "Alexei, allow me to introduce you to the Norns. This is Urd, Skuld, and Verthandi. Urd is Fate, Skuld is Being, and Verthandi is Necessity. "

Not sure what else to do, I fell back on my Kentucky upbringing, and turned to each in turn and said, "Pleased to meet you, ma'am."

They seemed shocked at being referred to as "Ma'am", but what the hell else was I supposed to do?

Odin seemed pleased as punch at my greeting. He now turned the tables and said, "Norns, allow me to introduce you to Alexei Addison."

That got the Norns steamed. Urd, the redhead, said, "Think you we do not know of this man's existence?"

"Have you a point here, Allfather?" This came from Skuld, the blonde. Through the process of elimination, that left Verthandi as the brunette. I know, I'm a regular detective.

Odin never changed his facial expression, although I could tell his was getting close to getting angry again. In a calm voice, he said, "Yes, Skuld, I have a point. Know you what this mortal has offered to do?"

All three of the women gave identical sighs. Urd answered. "Yes, Allfather, we know. We knew the second it happened."

This seemed to be what Odin was waiting for." Ah, yes… the second it happened. Why not *before* that?" he asked.

Urd tried to backtrack, but it was too little, too late.

Odin overrode her attempt to clarify things. "You knew the second it happened and not before because you know nothing about this man's future, is that not so?"

Urd looked positively livid and refused to speak. Finally, Verthandi answered. "It is true, Allfather, that in the skein of this mortal's life, the threads are very hard to see."

The other two Norns looked at Verthandi like she had slapped them in the face. She looked back calmly. "Well", she asked the others, "is that not so?"

Although they hated to admit it, the other two finally agreed that, as far as Alexei Addison was concerned, they were pretty much in the dark. That didn't exactly leave me feeling all that sure of myself.

Odin stepped into the breach. "Well. You can all see for yourselves what Alexei has done for us." He flapped a hand towards Loki and Fenrir. "Now, he says he is willing to remain here forever, guarding them. Now, I ask you, seems this fair to you?"

The Norns looked absolutely shocked to the core. Urd found her voice first. "*Fair*??? What care we for *fair*, Allfather? The universe is not a fair place, as well you know."

Odin nodded as if he expected that. "So true. Well, since the universe is not a fair place, I see no reason that we should triumph over Loki and Fenrir. In a *fair* universe, we would, but as you have pointed out..." He sighed and turned to face me. It's hard to wink with only one eye, but he pulled it off nicely.

"Alexei, free Loki and Fenrir."

I nodded, playing along. Since the Norns had no idea what I was going to do before I did it, they couldn't know if I was bluffing or nor. In a sad voice, I said, "As you say, Allfather. I had hoped to keep them fettered, but life isn't *fair...*" I raised my hands and the blue bands holding Loki and Fenrir began to dim.

Well, to say the next few seconds was loud and confusing would the understatement of the millennium.

After quite a bit of effort, we managed to calm the Norns down, all of whom looked like they had aged about twenty years in an instant. After everyone had gotten their breath back, Verthandi asked Odin, "What is it you want Allfather? These theatrics must have some reason."

Odin nodded to her respectfully. Of all the Norns, only Verthandi had kept her cool to any degree. "Verthandi, you see the quandary we have before us. Loki and Fenrir must remain as they are until Ragnarok for balance to be restored to the Nine Worlds. However, I will not have my son, so brutally ripped from his own world and thrust into this, to become their keeper from now until then. He has a life to lead, and I will see him lead it."

Verthandi looked at appraisingly. "I see what you ask, Allfather. I know not if it can be done. These are new waters for us all. Allow me to speak with my sisters and we shall see what we shall see."

Well, as far as vague answers went, that one was a dilly. I looked at Odin, but he shook his head and motioned for me to remain silent.

The Norns moved apart from the rest of us and stood talking. The talk got rather heated at points, and Urd especially seemed to be taking it hard. She gestured violently and spoke more loudly than the other two, but finally they seemed to come to a consensus. They walked back to where we stood.

It was Verthandi that spoke again. "It can be done, Allfather, but it will not be without pain."

Odin's brow clouded. "How much pain?"

"The pain of death, followed by the pain of birth. That is the cost. Know this, Allfather: the pain is not a punishment, it is merely necessary. We can do it no other way."

Odin looked at me for a moment and then said, "Alexei, the Norns can take this burden from you. They can take this power you possess into themselves, thereby keeping these two" he cast a contemptuous glance at Loki and Fenrir, "fettered until the proper time. You will be free to go on with your life. However, as you heard, there will be a great deal of pain involved. Pain unlike any you have ever had in your life. What say you? Would you have them do this?"

"Yes", I said immediately. "Do whatever it takes."

Odin smiled. "I expected nothing less from you. You are truly without fear."

I tried to smile back, but it was a poor thing. "Nope, I am truly full of fear. Fear of having to spend more than ten minutes with *those* assholes." Now I looked over at the captives. "Tyr was willing to lose a hand to get clear of just one of 'em. You can have both of mine if I can get out of here."

To my amazement, Tyr laughed. When he did, it lit up his whole face and transformed him into a totally different person. "I fully agree with him, Allfather", he said.

Since we were all in agreement, it was time to get down to business. The Norns surrounded me, placing their hands on my chest and back. I steeled myself, swearing that I wouldn't scream, that I wouldn't embarrass myself in front of the Aesir. In front of my family.

Just as I was about to begin, I felt another, much larger hand on my shoulder. I opened my eyes to see Thor standing behind Urd. He asked, "Cannot we help him in some way? Give him our strength, or at least share in his pain?"

The Norns looked shocked again, but after a silent look to one another, Urd said, "Yes to both. You can temporarily give him your strength, and you can help take some of his pain." She stopped, and looked at Thor in confusion. "Would you do such for this mortal?

Thor smiled. "No, I will not do such for this mortal. I will do such for my brother."

I beamed at him. "Thank you, big brother." I was about to say more when Heimdall stepped up and placed his hand on my other shoulder. Odin reached up and placed his hand on my cheek. Then Tyr stepped up and placed his single hand over Thor's. I looked at him questioningly. He smiled again. "No, Alexei, you are not my brother by blood or bone, but I would be honored if you would think of me as your brother in arms."

I was unable to speak. I nodded at all of them. I closed my eyes. It began.

I won't try to describe what happened to me, because there aren't words to do so. Suffice it to say; had it not been for the Aesir there to help me, I think I would have gone insane. I could have lived my life out, but only in a room with padded walls.

At some point, I lost consciousness.

Chapter Twenty-Three

When I came to, I was lying in a huge bed. Every single cell in my body seemed to have its own little catalogue of hurts, and each one was trying to report in at once. I just lay there, trying not to cry, for what seemed like forever. I heard someone enter the room, but when I tried to raise my head to see who it was, all my attempts at not crying shot out the window. I wept like a baby, and at that moment, I didn't give a damn if the entire host of the Einherjar here watching.

My visitor rushed up to my bed and I heard a familiar voice saying softly, 'No, no, you mustn't move, lie still. I will bring you something for the pain." A few seconds later, I felt a cool hand on my neck, helping me raise my head enough to drink from the cup at my lips. With the first mouthful I recognized the mead, and felt its potent power wash through me. Thinking I was good to go, I tried to sit up.

Again came the waterworks.

"No", said the soft voice again. "Even with the mead

of Frigg, you must lie still. Your injuries are far greater than you imagine.'

I was at least able to open my eyes now. I couldn't see very well at first, but slowly things came into focus. I looked up at my visitor and a smile made its way across my face.

"Sigyn? How are you?" I was appalled at the sound of my own voice. It was a husk of its former sound, like an old man.

Sigyn smiled brilliantly at me, which made me forget all about my voice for a second. She said, "I am fine, Alexei. It is you that needs care now."

I tried some of that old Alexei Addison charm. "I thought I told you to call me Alex" I said to her, giving her a wink.

She blushed, which I took to be a good sign. "Very well, *Alex*, how are you this day?"

I grinned. "Top of the world, ma'am." She raised an eyebrow. "Okay, maybe not top of the world, but I'm doing much better since I saw you."

The blush deepened. Yep, still had the charm.

"Well", she said, "it is a good thing that my presence pleases you, because I have asked to be your nurse while you recuperate."

My turn to blush. "Well, then I hope it's going to take a long time for me to get better", I said with another grin.

She turned serious. "It *will* take some time. You have been asleep for what you would reckon as three of your weeks."

Well, that got my attention. "I've been asleep for *three weeks???*"

Sigyn nodded. "You will need at least that much longer to regain your strength."

A thought hit me. "My parents! They'll be worried sick! Is there some way I can get a hold of them? I mean I guess the cell reception is crap here, but there must be something…"

Sigyn looked confused about the cell reception, but put my mind at ease when she said, "Heimdall has gone and seen your parents. They remain in the time bubble that they were placed in when all this began. You mustn't think of time here as it is in Midgard. Things are different."

"Heimdall said that my parents were put there for their protection." That led to another thought. "Loki! Fenrir! Are they fettered? What happened?"

There was a look of pain in Sigyn's eyes at the mention of her former husband. I fell all over myself apologizing, but she cut me off. "Loki was once an honorable creature. That is no more. The thing fettered on Lyngvi is my husband no more."

I couldn't help myself. "Does that mean you're…well…single?"

She gave me a narrow look. "Yes I suppose it does.

Not that you are in any shape to do anything about it."

Ouch. "Well, no, maybe not just yet, but give me some time..." I let my voice trail off playfully.

Sigyn made like she was going to slap me and then laughed. "You certainly have your father's nerve, I will give you that, Alex."

On impulse, I took her hand. My voice sober, I said, "All the things I said to you before we left Sigyn... I meant them. I want to know all about you. What you like, what you hate...everything. Is there a chance that maybe we could spend the next little while getting to know each other? I mean, since you're my nurse and all."

She smiled, and I felt my heart jump up into my throat and try to strangle me.

"We can spend this time learning all about one another, Alex, but you must understand..." She looked away.

"What?" I asked. "What is it?"

She looked back down at me and I could have sworn there was disappointment in her eyes. "Alex, you are the son of Odin, but you are mortal. You belong in Midgard. That is your life. There can be nothing more than friendship between us in the time you remain here. I am sorry."

I sighed. "Yeah. I'm sorry, too. I'm more than sorry." My voice was thick.

Sigyn stood suddenly. "You need rest, Alex. You

have been through much, and you need to allow yourself to heal." She turned to go.

"Wait", I said, "I need to know what happened. I understand that it's hard for you to talk about, but maybe Odin or one of the others could come and talk with me?"

She stood, indecisive. Finally, she said, "The Allfather said you would have questions when you awakened. I suppose you have done so. I shall see what I can do. Rest now, Alex." She gave me a final smile and left the room.

Nice, idiot, I raged at myself, *fall for a goddess. Why can't you just go after a cheerleader or something? As if someone like Sigyn would go for you. Real suave.*

I was still beating myself over the head when Odin walked in. He stood by my bed and smiled down at me. "You look well, my son."

I smiled back. "I feel better, Allfather. I mean, don't ask me to dance or anything, but I feel better than I did."

"I would not presume to tax your dancing abilities at the present time, Alexei. I understand you have some questions, however?"

"Yes, I do, Allfather. First and foremost: tell me that Loki and Fenrir are no longer a going concern."

He laughed. "You could very much say that, my son. They remain as you last saw them, fettered on Lyngvi. The Norns, in taking your power into themselves, are now able to keep them there without any fear of their escape." His face grew grim. "I looked into finding a serpent to restore Loki's punishment to what it was, but the cavern was too vast, and I could find none large enough to hang from the ceiling."

I thought about it for a few minutes and then said, "I wouldn't worry about it overmuch, Allfather. Loki may not have a serpent dripping poison on him, but he no longer has Sigyn, and his only companion is his demented son. I think they will run out of conversation material after they have devised all the ways they want me dead. I think they are suffering enough."

Odin was silent for a moment. "In another man, I would have taken that for weakness. But from you, I take it as yet another sign of your honor. It will be as you say. Although I doubt you will find any gratitude from either of them, I will inform them that their punishment will be no more than it is now."

I nodded, not knowing what else to say.

Odin sat with me for about an hour, and we exchanged pleasantries, but I could tell he had other things to do, so I made a point of giving out a bone-cracking yawn. (Which hurt like hell, by the way.)

Odin rose. "You are weary and still in much pain, my son. I will give you your rest. Sigyn has demanded that she nurse you. Simply call out and she will be here. Sleep now, and rest in the knowledge that your actions have saved the lives of more humans than you can ever imagine."

I really was falling asleep at this point. I mumbled

"Okay. Thank you…"

And then I knew nothing more than warm darkness.

Chapter Twenty-Four

I stayed under Sigyn's care for almost another month before I realized that I really did have to get home. Time may be different in Asgard, but the life I had been living before all this was still there, and I needed to find a way to ease back into it. I had no idea how to even begin that process.

Sigyn was as faithful to me as she had been to Loki. How that moron had managed to lose such a woman was beyond me. He deserved to be tied to a rock forever for that alone, in my book. Although she was there any time I needed anything, I could tell that I was becoming bothersome with my feelings for her. Hey, I couldn't help myself. You try and not fall in love with a beautiful goddess that takes care of your every need.

Heimdall came by almost every day, and we talked for hours. I taught him to play poker, once he managed to get us a pack of cards, and I soon learned that it was a huge hit in Valhalla. Imagining the Einherjar playing high-stakes poker always gave me the giggles, for some reason. Thor came by from time to time and, with the air of a man doing another man a huge favor, told me I could borrow his DVD player, T.V., and collection of DVDs. I thanked him sincerely, since I knew how much it meant to him. I told him I was more of a reader, and asked if he might be able to run me down some books somewhere. He assured me he would, and left. I got the feeling he was tickled pink that I enjoyed the printed word to T.V. He brought back a couple of huge tomes bound in leather. They were written in Old Norse, and worse, Runic, but I was happy to see I could still speak and read the language. I wondered if that would fade when I went home.

Finally, the day came when I was ready to go. A huge feast was laid on for me in Valhalla the night before, and I came close to losing all the health I had managed to gain back in one night of drinking and card playing with the Einherjar, who were just as balls-to-the-wall as ever. Never play Texas Hold 'Em with the slain warriors of Valhalla. Just *don't*. I woke up the next morning feeling like I had gone ten rounds with a bull, but it was a good feeling, in a weird way.

Everyone was dressed in their Sunday best as I made my way through Asgard and toward Bifrost. Just short of the Rainbow Bridge stood the Aesir. I shook hands formally with those I hadn't had a chance to get to know better, and received a good-natured punch in the shoulder from Thor that caused my arm to go numb for about an hour. Tyr took my hand and told me to remember his vow on Lyngvi, that I was his brother in arms, and to call on him anytime I wished. I thanked him again and told him I would.

Odin and Frigg were standing at the edge of Bifrost.

Odin embraced me and looked me deep in the eyes. "I have often wondered through the years if my indiscretion on Midgard would haunt me. It shamed me, for the love I have for Frigg is boundless. But now I see that perhaps it was not merely the weakness of the flesh that drove me to that act, for I had never done so before, and have never done so since. I do not seek and excuse for my actions, for Frigg has forgiven me long ago for that night, but I see in it now something more than simple lust."

"I now believe that that night, that girl, all the years and generations that have occurred since, were all leading up to you, Alexei. If you were not who you are, the Nine Worlds would now be destroyed. It is not only that you are my son that I say this. I mean if you were not the kind of man you are, Alexei... the horrors that you have kept from happening... and that so few know... it shames me that your name is not known throughout the universe, my son."

I smiled, embarrassed right to the roots of my hair. Trying to play it off, I said, "It's all right Allfather. When I get my degree, I'll just paint 'Alex Addison, Attorney-at-Law and Savior of the Universe' on my window."

Odin growled at me and pulled me in for another bone-crusher of an embrace. He stepped back, his eye a little moist.

Frigg was her usual graceful self, and she embraced me in turn. Smiling sweetly up into my face, she said, "Alexei, I have no right to, but if you would permit it, I would like to be able to call you my son, as well. It would be an honor."

I was floored. This was the goddess I figured would gut me the first chance she got when I arrived in Asgard. Stuttering, I managed to get out, "The honor would be mine. You are too kind to me, too kind by far. I thank you… mother." Her smile was worth everything that had happened to me since Heimdall had jerked me out of Midgard.

Speak of the devil; here came the big lug now. Tossing his arm around me, he asked, "Ready, little brother?"

I looked back at the host of gods and goddesses, warriors and friends. With a sigh, I said, "Sure thing, big bro. Let's get this show on the road. I've still got to study for finals."

Heimdall was nobody's fool, and he was the Watchman of the Gods, after all. He caught on to my melancholy right off the bat.

"You're disappointed at not seeing Sigyn before you left, aren't you?"

I tried to shrug it off, but thought, *what the hell.*

"Yeah, I am, a little. I mean, she made it pretty clear the boundaries of our relationship, but I guess I at least deserved a good-bye from her." It was hard to keep the bitterness from my voice.

Heimdall nodded. "Listen, little brother, Sigyn can't be involved with a mortal in Asgard, it just isn't possible. It wasn't that she didn't care about you, it's just that some rules can't be broken."

"Not even for the guy that saved the known universe?" I asked a little angrily.

Heimdall shook his head. "Nope, not even for the guy that saved the known universe. Jeez, I hope you don't let that go to your head."

I rolled my eyes. "Heaven forbid."

We started our walk back through Bifrost, and I took one last look back at Asgard. The dim half-light and endless snow depressed me once again. As we walked, I asked Heimdall, "Do you think the sun will ever shine in Asgard again? Or that the Einherjar we lost will return?"

We walked on in silence so long that I didn't think he was going to answer me. Finally, he said, "I don't know Alexei. Maybe the time of the Norse gods has passed forever. Maybe that's how it should be." He looked into the distance, wistful. "I would like to see the sun in Asgard one last time before the end, though."

We walked the rest of the way in silence. After a while I could see the colors surrounding us again and we soon stood right where we started from, the middle of the University of Kentucky football stadium.

I glanced at Heimdall. "Is this the only place Bifrost opens up, big brother? Because I bet the Norsemen back in the day had one hell of a time getting here."

He grinned at me. "Bite me, little brother. There were Norsemen on this continent half a century before any of those other European fops so much as saw the place."

We stepped out of Bifrost into the cold night of Kentucky. I looked at myself and gaped. I was wearing the exact same clothing I had been wearing the night Heimdall had come to get me. Looking at him, I saw he was, too. I also noticed that he was a full head taller than me again, as well. Great. More midget jokes were in my immediate future.

Looking around, I said, "You know, if I didn't know any better, I'd swear that this is the exact same night you came and got me."

He grinned again. "It is."

I looked at him, dumbfounded. "*What?*"

"This is the exact same night I first saw you. In fact, this is the exact same minute we left Midgard. If we had been here a second sooner, we would have passed ourselves going in. How's *that* for a mind scramble?"

I made a long series of incomprehensible sounds before I could manage words. Finally, I got out, "How the *fuck* did you guys pull that off?"

"Well, we had to haggle with the Norns a bit, but since they hadn't foreseen any of this, they caved pretty easy. All is well, little brother."

It took me a second, but then the light came on in my head. "My dorm…it's fine? I mean, none of the shit Loki did…?"

"In essence, Loki didn't do it. By re-fettering him and having the Norns restore balance, you have everything just as it was."

"Jesus! That means that Isaac Macintyre... he's...?"

"He should be getting high and listening to Imogen Heap on his IPod." Heimdall laughed.

I laughed right along with him. After we had gotten that out of our system, I said, "Well, Heimdall... or sorry, *Henry*... it's been groovy." I stuck my hand out, but he just looked at it. "Okay... um, what am I missing?"

He shook his head in mock disgust. "Damn near two months among the Norse, and you haven't learned a damn thing about hospitality. Isn't this the part where you invite me to your room for a beer?"

I slapped myself on the forehead. "Dammit, I'm sorry. A lot on my mind, I guess. Heimdall, Watchman of the Gods, would you do me the honor of accompanying me to my meager abode to partake in the watered-down piss that we pitiful mortals call beer?"

He grinned and said, "Why, thank you, Alexei; I would be honored to do so."

We walked back across campus to my dorm. I was again amazed at how *small* everything seemed now, with Heimdall as my basis for comparison. We entered my building and headed down my hallway. We stopped just outside my dorm room, looking at each other.

"I don't remember leaving the radio on when we left. Did I?" I asked.

Heimdall shook his massive head. "Nope, there wasn't a thing on in there when we left here. Sounds to me like somebody decided to crash into your room, little brother."

I felt myself getting pissed. I knew that I wasn't as big a bad-ass now as I had been in Asgard, by god, I was bad enough for any of *these* little punks.

"Excuse me just a second, Heimdall. I've got to take out some trash before I invite you in."

"No problem."

I threw open the door and launched myself into the room, ready to give somebody the scare of their life. I skidded to a stop when I saw my intruder was blonde, about six feet tall, wearing skin-tight jeans and a tee-shirt cut off to her midriff. She was facing away from me, dancing to Lady GaGa of all things. I could let her taste in music go, so long as she kept dancing like that.

It was hard to talk with all the saliva in my mouth dried up, but I managed to get out, "Excuse me, ma'am?"

Then she turned around.

"SIGYN???"

With a gleeful shriek, she jumped across the room. I caught her in mid-leap, and she locked her legs around me. I started to ask what in the hell was going on, but I suddenly found myself very, very busy kissing a Norse goddess. When we finally broke from the kiss, I turned, still holding Sigyn. I looked at Heimdall.

"Just what in the *fuck* is going on here?"

Heimdall looked confused. "Well", he said, "it looks to me like you were kissing Sigyn. Of course, all I could see was the back of your head, but if you weren't kissing her, I'm damned if *I* know what you were doing."

"You know what I mean!!! What was all that 'a goddess can't be with a mortal in Asgard; it's against the rules' shit???"

Heimdall looked around theatrically. "Are we in Asgard?"

I started grinning. Then I started laughing. Pretty soon I found myself kissing Sigyn again. Finally, Heimdall said, "Okay, enough. Yuck, already. Get a room, you two."

Taking a second to catch my breath, I looked at him and said, "I've *got* a room, bro, and you're currently *in* it."

With a final smile, he said, "I'm gone. I'll see you around, little brother."

He took off, and I could hear him thumping down the hallway. I kicked the door to my room shut. Before she could glue her mouth to mine again, I looked deep into Sigyn's eyes and said, "My momma's just gonna love *you*."

Epilogue

"Hey, Daddy, can I open the mail?"

I turned from the case file I was reading to see my
six year old holding a pile of mail. It was his newest
thing, getting the mail. It was cute, but since I get a lot
of official court documents in my mailbox, it was kind
of important that I check just what Henry was going
through when he opened the mail.

"Sure, kiddo. Why don't you come over here and
we'll open it together?"

"Sure Daddy. Hey Mommy, do you wanna open the
mail with me 'n Daddy?"

Sigyn walked into the room with a dab of flour on
her nose. She was making a cake. And sweet *lord*, could
she make a dab of flour sexy. She grinned at us and said,
"No, you boys go ahead and open it. If I get anything
good, let me know, all right?" Then she walked back
into the kitchen.

I tore my eyes off the spectacle of my wife walking

into the kitchen. Turning my attention back to Henry, I said, "All right, chief, what do we have here?"

As we went through the mail together, I heard Henry mumbling under his breath. I could catch an occasional word. It was Old Norse. I hadn't forgotten it when I had returned, and it was Sigyn's first language, of course. Henry had grown up around it.

"Whatcha sayin' there, chief?"

Henry looked at me and said, in perfect Old Norse, "I'm just praying to the gods, Daddy. I pray to them every day."

I felt a lump in my throat. In Old Norse, I replied, "That's good son. You go right ahead."

We rummaged through the mail until I came upon a small envelope about the size of a postcard. I looked at the front, and all it said was "Alexei Addison and Family". There was no return address, and no postmark. Odd.

I opened the envelope and peered inside. It was a picture. I slid the picture out into my hands and nearly dropped it. In a weak voice I said "Sigyn?" I was so breathless that Henry ran to the door and hollered, "Mommy, Daddy wants you. He's got a picture or somethin' he wants you to see."

Sigyn was walking back into the room, something that usually captured all of my attention, but not this time. This time all I could do was stare at the picture in my hand. A picture of Asgard, as I remembered it, with one major exception: the sun was shining. On the back of the picture Heimdall had written just two sentences:

"All present and accounted for here. Give my nephew a kiss for me. —H"

Afterword

When most people think of the Norsemen, they instantly conjure up visions of blood-soaked raids on innocent monasteries and villages. And while this was a part of the Norse culture, it was only a tiny fraction. Norsemen were the first to build boats capable of crossing the North Atlantic, and it was a Norseman, Leif Erickson, that discovered North America five hundred years before Columbus. The term "Viking" referred to a small section of the Norse populace. The word itself derives from the Norse word "Vik", which meant "River". So, to go "Viking" was to go on a river voyage. These "Vikings" *were* a rather blood-thirsty lot, but it is unfair to judge the whole of the Norse world by a small segment of its people.

I'm sure that the various names of the assorted Norse cast and crew were bothersome to many of you, as you tried to puzzle out how the hell to even pronounce their names. However, rest assured that each one of the individuals within (except Alexi, or course) are based in fact and each of them are exactly what they have been portrayed as. I should know, I pray to them each day.

Do yourself a favor and hit the internet, or if you are truly hardcore, find a local library, and study the Norse people and their ways. You will be pleasantly surprised at how they are like us. Chances are you've got yourself a Viking in the woodpile.

-September 19, 2013 3:47 A.M.

For Lu. Tha gael agam ort, mo chridhe..

Ryan S. Pack was born and raised in Eastern Kentucky. He lives there still with his wife LuAnn and their four children. He was an Emergency Medical Technician for fifteen years before an injury ended that career. He has since spent his time in and out of college, where he remains one credit shy of a degree, and writing what he refers to as "My Ramblings". My Father's Son is his first novel.

All the work contained herein is a work of fiction. All the characters are part of the author's imagination. All places, with the exception of the University of Kentucky and Columbia, Kentucky are likewise fictitious. With those two exceptions, the author has taken liberties with the geography. Having said that, to those of you who believe, Asgard and all its populace are as real as the planet we live on. I proudly count myself among that number, as does my son.